OTIS SPOFFORD

OTHER YEARLING BOOKS YOU WILL ENJOY:

Mitch and Amy, BEVERLY CLEARY
Socks, BEVERLY CLEARY
Henry and the Paper Route, BEVERLY CLEARY
The Mouse and the Motorcycle, BEVERLY CLEARY
Emily's Runaway Imagination, BEVERLY CLEARY
Henry and Ribsy, BEVERLY CLEARY
Beezus and Ramona, BEVERLY CLEARY
Ellen Tebbits, BEVERLY CLEARY
Henry and the Clubhouse, BEVERLY CLEARY
Henry Huggins, BEVERLY CLEARY

YEARLING BOOKS/YOUNG YEARLINGS/YEARLING CLASSICS are designed especially to entertain and enlighten young people. Patricia Reilly Giff, consultant to this series, received the bachelor's degree from Marymount College. She holds the master's degree in history from St. John's University, and a Professional Diploma in Reading from Hofstra University. She was a teacher and reading consultant for many years, and is the author of numerous books for young readers.

For a complete listing of all Yearling titles, write to
Dell Readers Service, P.O. Box 1045,
South Holland, IL 60473.

OTIS SPOFFORD

by BEVERLY CLEARY

Illustrated by Louis Darling

A YEARLING BOOK

Published by
Dell Publishing
a division of
Bantam Doubleday Dell Publishing Group, Inc.
666 Fifth Avenue
New York, New York 10103

Yearling ® TM 913705, Dell Publishing Co., Inc.

ISBN: 0-440-46651-2

Reprinted by arrangement with William Morrow and Company, Inc.
Printed in the United States of America
May 1980

20   19   18   17   16   15   14   13
CW

Contents

OTIS SPOFFORD

CHAPTER ONE

Otis Gets His Man

THERE was nothing Otis Spofford liked better than stirring up a little excitement. Otis was a medium-sized boy with reddish-brown hair, freckles, and ears that stuck out. He often wore a leather jacket with a rabbit's foot tied to the zipper, and he always laced his shoes with the kind of laces that glow in the dark—pink for the right shoe and green for the left.

Otis found it hard to stir up any excitement around home. He was sure it would be easier if he lived in a house with a yard to play in, like the other boys and girls in Room Eleven at Rosemont School. Instead, he lived with his mother, Valerie Todd Spofford, in an apartment. Mrs. Spofford was away from home most of the time teaching ballet and tap-dancing lessons at the Spofford School of the Dance over the Payless Drugstore.

Otis wished his mother had more time to spend at home, so that Mrs. Brewster, the manager of the apartment house, would not have to keep her eye on him. Mrs. Spofford was never very cross with Otis for wanting to stir up a little excitement, but Mrs. Brewster made it plain that she did not like dirt, dogs, or noise, and that she stood for no nonsense from boys.

School, however, was different. Except for

learning things, Otis liked school. He could find so many ways to stir up excitement.

Once a week Otis's teacher, Mrs. Gitler, took her class to the auditorium for folk dancing. Otis was the only member of the class who did not like this period.

I'd rather play dodge ball any day, he always thought as they marched down the hall. I see enough dancing at the Spofford School of the Dance.

The class had learned several dances, like "Stupid One Hopping on One Foot" and "I Lost My Way in the Gooseberry Bushes," but for the past few weeks they had been practicing a Mexican folk dance for the *fiesta* Rosemont School was planning for a Parent Teacher Association meeting. Each class in the school was to give a Mexican dance. Afterwards, the mothers in the P.T.A. would sell cookies and punch to raise money for visual aids for the school.

Otis was not the least bit excited about the *fiesta*. He was sure the P.T.A. would rather see a good ball game.

There were three more boys than girls in the class. This meant that two boys had to dance together, one of them, against his wishes, taking the part of a girl. The third boy danced alone. Otis was usually the third boy. No one wanted him for a partner, because he liked to hop on his right foot when he was supposed to hop on his left. This was hard on his partner's toes. He didn't care if no one wanted to dance with him, and today as he went through the steps alone, he amused himself by dancing stiff-legged.

Mrs. Gitler stopped the phonograph. "Otis, be a gentleman," she said.

"Mrs. Gitler, I don't see why I have to be in the old *fiesta*," complained Otis. "There are too many boys in the class anyway."

"Me, too," said Stewy Hicks promptly.

Leave it to old Stewy, thought Otis. That was the trouble with Stewy. He liked to get in on whatever excitement Otis was stirring up.

To Otis's surprise, Mrs. Gitler smiled and said, "I have a different plan for the three extra boys."

Now what? wondered Otis, thinking he might get into something worse than folk dancing.

"We are going to have a bullfight in the center of the circle of dancers. One boy will be a toreador and the other two will wear a bull costume." Mrs. Gitler paused while the class laughed at the thought of two boys dressed up like a bull. "At the end of the dance, when the toreador wins and the bull falls down, the girls will all take flowers out of their hair and toss them at the toreador."

Otis was pleased with this idea. He could see himself dressed up like a bullfighter, waving his red cape in front of the bull and stepping nimbly aside when the bull charged at him. He would bow to the crowd while the girls showered him with flowers and the audience cheered. Maybe he was going to like the *fiesta* after all.

Mrs. Gitler spoiled his daydream by saying, "Otis, since you do not care about folk dancing, you may be half the bull."

The class laughed. "The front half or the back half?" Otis wanted to know.

"The front half," answered Mrs. Gitler. "Stewart, you may be the other half. George, you may be the toreador."

Otis could see that George felt pretty good about being the toreador. Oh, well, thought Otis, being the front half of the bull was not so bad. It was better than folk dancing, and he and Stewy ought to have fun.

Then Mrs. Gitler had the three boys practice bullfighting. Stewy put his hands on Otis's hips and the two boys charged at George, who twirled an imaginary cape in front of them. When George

pretended to stab the bull with a sword, Otis and Stewy fell to the floor.

"All right, Otis," said Mrs. Gitler. "I don't think it is necessary for the bull to die with his front feet in the air. Falling to the floor is enough."

Otis lay on the floor and watched George bow, as the girls pretended to throw flowers at him. He thought George looked very pleased with himself.

When the bell rang for recess, Otis followed George around, singing:

"Toreador-a,
Don't spit on the floor-a.
Use the cuspidor-a,
That's what it's for-a."

Of course Stewy joined in. Otis was a little disappointed when George only grinned and said, "Aw, keep quiet."

When the afternoon of the *fiesta* finally arrived, all Rosemont School bustled with excitement. The teachers wore white blouses, long full skirts, and flowers in their hair. Even Mr. Howe, the prin-

cipal, wore a Mexican hat and a red sash. While the ladies of the P.T.A. worked to get the cookie and punch booths ready on the playground, the teachers worked to get the children ready inside the classrooms.

Mrs. Gitler's face was flushed. She was hurriedly fastening pa-

per stripes down the legs of the boys' jeans with
Scotch tape. Otis and Stewy already wore the leg
parts of their costume, which looked like pajama
pants made out of gunny sacks. They were practicing walking like a bull. Otis had worked out a
few variations, like skipping backwards. He could
hardly wait to get the top part of the costume.

The girls, who were wearing white blouses and
full skirts with crepe-paper ruffles basted around
the hems, were busy pinning flowers in their hair.

"Now, Otis, I want you to behave yourself,"
said Mrs. Gitler, as she started to tie crepe-paper
sashes around the boys' waists.

Otis, who had not done a thing yet, felt a little
guilty. How did Mrs. Gitler know that he was
looking around for a little excitement to stir up?

Otis watched Ellen Tebbits tug at a lock of her
hair, and he heard her say to Austine Allen, "I
wish my hair would hurry up and grow long
enough for pigtails." Then she tipped her head

back and shook her hair so it brushed against the back of her neck. "It feels longer when I do this," she explained.

Otis enjoyed teasing Ellen more than anybody. He did not know what it was about her that made him feel that way. Maybe it was because she was so neat and clean and well behaved. Or maybe it was because he knew he could always make her mad. Now he tipped his head back in imitation of Ellen. "I wish my hair would grow long enough for pigtails," he said in a squeaky voice.

"Oh, for goodness' sakes," snapped Ellen.

"Oh, for gunny sacks," said Otis. He was pleased when everyone laughed. "Oh, for gunny sacks," he repeated, to get another laugh.

Then Otis stopped teasing Ellen, because the door opened and George walked into the room wearing his toreador suit. Otis stared with the rest of the class. There were no jeans with paper stripes for George. He was wearing black velvet knee pants and a velvet hat that Otis had seen one of the P.T.A. ladies making out of an old dress. Around his shoulders was a splendid cape that no one would ever guess had once been the skirt of someone's evening dress. Stuck through his green sash, he wore a short wooden sword. George did not walk. He swaggered. "*Adios,*" he said grandly.

"*Chili con carne,*" answered Otis, using the only Spanish phrase he knew. He had learned it from cans which his mother sometimes opened for lunch when she was in a hurry.

"He sure thinks he's smart," observed Stewy.

"I wish Mrs. Gitler would hurry up and let us have the top of our bull costume," remarked Otis, who did not like to see George getting all the attention.

But Mrs. Gitler was in no hurry to have a four-legged animal running around her classroom. Otis grew more impatient as she finished the boys' sashes and began to hand out tambourines to the girls. When she ran out of tambourines, she distributed old milk cartons filled with pebbles. The lucky girls with tambourines banged them happily, while the girls who had to take milk cartons sulked. Otis noticed that Ellen, who was one of the best pupils in his mother's dancing classes, had a tambourine and was practicing steps she had learned at the Spofford School of the Dance.

While Otis was trying to think of a way to tease Ellen some more, George swaggered by and looked scornfully at Otis's and Stewy's burlap trousers. "*Adios,*" he scoffed.

"Old Fancypants," muttered Otis, and began to sing *Toreador-a, don't spit on the floor-a.*

"All right, Otis and Stewart," said Mrs. Gitler. "You may go to the auditorium for the rest of your costume."

"Oh, boy!" shouted Otis, as the two boys raced out of the room.

"And no running in the halls," called Mrs. Gitler. Of course, they paid no attention.

The P.T.A. ladies helped Otis and Stewy into the top of the costume. Otis's end had a head with a fine pair of horns, made out of rolled-up cardboard. Stewy's half had a tail made of rope fringed at the end. The head was fastened to a stick that Otis held inside the bull's burlap body. It was dark inside the bull, but Otis could see where he was going, because there was a peephole under the bull's jaw.

Otis was satisfied when the ladies laughed at

him and Stewy in their costume. He made the bull nod its head, paw the ground, and run out of the auditorium and down the hall. Now maybe he could stir up a little excitement.

The class shouted with laughter when they saw the animal. Otis felt someone pat his head, which looked like the bull's shoulder from the outside, and heard Tommy say, "How's old Ferdinand?" Through his peephole Otis saw that George paid no attention. He was too busy twirling his cape.

"All right, boys and girls," said Mrs. Gitler. "Let's get in line. It's time for the parade. Come on, George, you go first. Bull, you're next. Find your partners, everybody."

Otis could not resist poking George in the seat of his velvet pants with the bull's horns. Old Fancypants, he thought.

"Cut that out," said George.

"Come along, people," said Mrs. Gitler, as she led the way out of the classroom.

All the classes in the school paraded around the playground, which was supposed to be a village square. The mothers sat on the bleachers on three sides of the square. The baseball backstop, covered with crepe paper, was on the fourth side. In front of it was a platform with several chairs, a phonograph, and a microphone.

When Otis saw the audience, he was carried away. Now he could stir up a little excitement. He made the bull nod and bow and paw the ground. When everyone laughed, he made the bull wave. This was difficult to do, because he had to stand on one foot while he waved the other. The audience laughed harder. Otis began to skip and Stewy had to follow.

"You cut that out," ordered George. "You're supposed to walk behind me."

Otis lowered the bull's head and started to charge, but by that time the class had come to its section of chairs in front of the bleachers. Everyone sat down except Otis and Stewy, who had to stand up.

Mrs. Gitler leaned over and whispered to Otis through his peephole. "Some of the mothers can't see over you. Maybe you boys had better wait behind the backstop until our turn. We come on after the kindergarten does its Mexican cowboy dance." The bull trotted behind the backstop, where Otis could hear the principal welcoming the mothers.

"George sure thinks he's something," said Stewy.

"Who does he think he is, giving us orders?" Otis wanted to know. He rubbed his ears where the burlap scratched him, and thought what a good joke it would be on George if he could think of a way to keep him from being the whole show.

"We ought to do something about him," said Stewy.

"I'm thinking," said Otis. The bull leaned against

the backstop while the president of the P.T.A. welcomed the mothers. "Hey, I know what," exclaimed Otis, and whispered to Stewy.

"That's a super idea," agreed Stewy. "Let's go."

The boys took off the top half of their costume and hid it under a pile of papers. Crouching low, they ran out from behind the backstop and around to some empty seats in the sixth-grade section. Everyone was listening to a member of the school board welcome the mothers, and no one paid any attention to Otis and Stewy, who were careful to sit very still.

They continued to sit still while the kindergarten did its Mexican cowboy dance. They scarcely breathed as they watched Mrs. Gitler go behind the backstop and look around for the missing bull. They slid down in their chairs and grinned at each other when their whole class stood up to look for them. Otis was especially pleased with George's worried look. This ought to show him that without a bull to fight he didn't amount to much.

When the audience became restless because of the delay, Otis and Stewy exchanged glances. "Now," whispered Otis, and the two boys began to stamp their feet and clap their hands. The older boys around them joined in, while others began to whistle for the show to go on. Soon all the boys in the school were stamping, clapping, or whistling. Otis and Stewy exchanged satisfied looks. They had started even more noise than they expected.

"We'll let them look a little longer," said Otis.

"Quiet!" roared the principal into the microphone. When the noise subsided he said, "I am disappointed to learn that the boys of Rosemont School do not know how to behave like gentlemen."

"Hey, look," whispered Stewy. "They're beginning without us."

The class was moving toward the center of the playground. This was not part of the plan.

"We better get going," Otis told Stewy as they started back where they belonged. They pulled out the top half of the bull costume and scrambled into it. They were not going to miss performing in the bull suit if they could help it.

"All right," snapped Mrs. Gitler, when she saw them. "You boys get in place in a hurry. I'll deal with you later."

"Come on! Hurry up!" ordered George.

"Moo," answered Otis.

When Mrs. Gitler started the phonograph, George swaggered onto the playground with the bull tagging along behind. The rest of the class followed and took positions on the circle painted on the cement. Then they began to dance. Partners faced each other, slid to the right, stamped their

feet, and slid to the left. The girls jingled their tambourines and rattled their milk cartons in time to the music.

Through his peephole Otis could see George standing in the center, waving his cape. Suddenly he had a wonderful idea. It was so good he wondered why he hadn't thought of it sooner. Now he would really stir up something. "Hey, Stewy," he whispered. "We're going to catch it anyway. Let's have some fun."

"O.K.," agreed Stewy.

Otis whispered his plan and Stewy snorted with laughter. "Let's start with chasing our tail," directed Otis. "I mean your tail," he added, since the tail really belonged to Stewy.

As Otis and Stewy ran around in a circle, the audience began to laugh. Otis could see the class did not like having people laugh while they were

dancing. Several got out of step and had to hop on one foot to get in step again.

Now Otis and Stewy lay down on the cement. The audience laughed harder. George advanced, scowling and waving his cape. Otis gave the signal, and he and Stewy stood up and began to skip backwards.

"Cut out the funny business," said George. "My cape is supposed to make you mad."

Otis lowered the bull's head and charged. George stepped aside as the bull rushed through the cape. Then Otis turned sharply and poked George in the seat of the pants with his horns.

"Hey," yelled George, and the audience howled. "You cut that out. You're not supposed to do that."

Enjoying himself thoroughly, Otis skipped merrily around the circle of dancers and prepared to charge again, while the girls, banging their tambourines and rattling their milk cartons, danced around their partners.

Boy, he's really mad now, thought Otis, as he watched George through his peephole. This is really good.

Once more George flapped his cape. The bull ran past it, and Otis started to poke the toreador again. But this time George was too quick. He pulled his sword out of his belt and gave the back end of the bull a good hard swat with the side of the wooden blade.

"Yow!" came a voice from the middle of the bull. The toreador swatted again.

"Yow!" yelled the middle of the bull again. The audience screamed with laughter. By this time every one of the dancers was out of step.

"Hey, Otis," said Stewy. "Let's cut this out. That hurt."

"Too late now," answered Otis, lowering the head for another charge. He was having too much fun to stop now. There was nothing for Stewy to do but follow.

This time Otis managed to poke the toreador again. George grabbed the bull by the tail and swatted with his sword.

"Ouch," yelled Stewy. "Otis Spofford, you cut this out."

"Hang on," ordered Otis. "We'll get him this time."

"I'll get *you* for this," retorted Stewy. "Just because you're the front end . . ."

The bull jerked its tail out of the toreador's hands and charged so fast that George did not have a chance to get out of the way.

George tripped, Otis pushed so hard that he bent the bull's horns, and the toreador lay flat on the cement. Otis planted his right foot in the middle of the toreador's green sash, while the audience clapped and shouted. Delighted with the commotion he was causing, Otis made the bull bow to the right and to the left. He felt George struggling to get up, so he pushed his foot down harder as he bowed once more to the audience.

The class gave up trying to dance. Everyone stopped to watch the victorious bull. "Aren't we supposed to throw our flowers?" asked one of the girls.

"You let me up!" George wiggled under the bull's foot.

"You just wait," muttered Stewy, inside the burlap behind Otis.

The girls pulled the flowers out of their hair and tossed them at the bull.

"Otis Spofford!" hissed Mrs. Gitler.

Otis could not resist one more bow. Then he took his foot off the toreador and the bull trotted out of the ring in a shower of petals. George got up and angrily brushed himself off.

Mrs. Gitler was waiting for Otis and Stewy. She snatched off the top of their costume. "Now you boys sit on those two chairs and don't you dare move until the program is over," she said grimly.

Otis was not worried. He knew that Mrs. Gitler never stayed cross with him very long. Satisfied with the excitement he had caused, he took a deep breath of fresh air. It had been hot and stuffy inside the bull.

"It was all his idea," growled Stewy, rubbing the seat of his pants.

"I'll get him for that," said George.

"Quiet!" ordered Mrs. Gitler. "Otis Spofford,

one of these days you are going to go too far."

"Who, me?" asked Otis innocently.

"Yes, you," said his teacher. "Some day, Otis, you are going to get your come-uppance."

"What's 'come-uppance'?" asked Otis.

"You'll find out," answered Mrs. Gitler.

"That old Otis Spofford, spoiling our dance!" said Ellen, as she slid past him to sit down.

Otis knew he was safe for a while. There was nothing the two boys could do but glower at him for the rest of the program. Stewy did manage a couple of sideways kicks, but that was all.

Otis decided he might as well leave as soon as the program ended. There was really no reason why he should stay around for punch and cookies. But when the time came, the three boys and their teacher were surrounded by smiling mothers.

Now I'll catch it, thought Otis. Oh, well, it was worth it. The way things had turned out, it had been even more fun than a ball game.

"What a clever act you planned," exclaimed one of the mothers to Mrs. Gitler.

"And so original, having the bull win," added another.

Mrs. Gitler looked startled. She opened her mouth to say something, but no words came out.

Well, how do you like that? thought Otis, laughing to himself. They think that was the way the bullfight was supposed to be. Boy, oh, boy, is this a good joke!

"We enjoyed it so much," murmured some more mothers.

This time Mrs. Gitler managed to smile as she said, "Why . . . uh . . . thank you."

"I don't know when I've laughed so hard," said another mother.

"I am so glad you enjoyed our program," Mrs. Gitler responded graciously.

"But, Mrs. Gitler," protested George, "I was supposed to . . ."

"Never mind now, George," said Mrs. Gitler. "We'll talk about it later."

"But . . ." said George.

"I said *never mind*," repeated Mrs. Gitler.

"You heard what the teacher said," Otis put in.

"I guess you think you're pretty smart," muttered George.

"Well, aren't I?" asked Otis cockily.

"You just wait," said Stewy.

Otis saw his mother coming through the crowd. She put her arm around him and said, "You performed beautifully. I was proud of my boy."

Otis grinned at the other two boys, who glared back.

"I must hurry or I'll be late for my ballet class," Mrs. Spofford said. "Be a good boy and go right home."

"Sure," answered Otis, thinking his mother would be surprised if she knew just how quickly he planned to go home.

When Mrs. Spofford left, Otis felt there was no reason to hang around any longer. He ducked out of the crowd and headed for home as fast as he could run.

Two pairs of feet came pounding down the sidewalk after him. "You just wait," yelled Stewy and George.

"Toreador-a," sang Otis at the top of his voice. After all, he had a good head start.

CHAPTER TWO

Otis Takes Aim

OTIS did not know what it was about Friday morning that made him feel he had to stir up some excitement. Maybe it was the crispness of the air. Maybe it was knowing the next day was Saturday. Or maybe it was because Mrs. Brewster had kept her eye on him for such a long time the afternoon before.

First of all, Otis decided to go to school by way

of Tillamook Street. When he saw Ellen Tebbits come out of her house, he chased her all the way to school. This made her hot and cross. "You . . . stop . . . chasing me, Otis . . . Spofford," she panted, when she was safe on the school grounds.

"You . . . stop . . . chasing me," mimicked Otis.

Ellen stamped her foot.

After the first bell rang, Otis saw Austine Allen come running down the street as fast as she could go. Her face was red and both her hair ribbons had come untied. When she had caught her breath, she said crossly to Ellen, "You said you were coming by for me this morning. I waited and waited until I was almost tardy."

"I couldn't," said Ellen. "That old Otis chased me." Both girls glared at Otis as they hurried into the classroom.

Otis did not go in with the others. Instead, he stood just outside the door of Room Eleven to wait for the tardy bell to ring. He knew this worried everyone in the class, because they were anxious to be one hundred per cent on time. When the bell buzzed through the halls, he waited two and seven-eighths seconds before he stepped into the room. His timing was perfect. The bell stopped ringing just as he came through the door.

Mrs. Gitler looked at Otis. "Remember what I said about come-uppance," she warned, and went on writing arithmetic problems on the blackboard.

Otis knew that when he wanted to be he was the smartest boy in arithmetic in Mrs. Gitler's room. This morning he decided he wanted to be. He worked his problems quickly, not because he cared about finishing first, but because he wanted Mrs. Gitler to scold him for not working. Then he planned to drop a sheet of perfect problems on her desk and wait for her look of amazement when she saw that he had not only completed his work but had not made a single mistake.

As soon as Otis finished his problems he looked around for a good way to waste time. Maybe there was something interesting in his pockets. Besides a tangle of string, rubber bands, and bent paper clips, he found a rabbit's foot with most of the fur worn off, a couple of old milk-bottle caps he carried in case he wanted to start a collection some day, a yo-yo with a tangled string, and a clove of garlic he had picked up from the drain board at home for no reason at all.

Otis studied the clove of garlic, but he could not think of anything to do with it, so he put it back in his pocket. Then he tried to unsnarl the yo-yo string but soon lost interest. Wishing he could think of something more interesting, he tore off a corner of his arithmetic paper, put it in his mouth, and chewed it. Then he blew it out and watched it turn and twist as it floated through the air and landed on the back of Stewy's neck. Otis quickly bent over his work before Stewy turned around.

"Stewart, have you finished your problems?" asked the teacher.

"No, Mrs. Gitler." Stewy wiped the back of his neck with his hand.

"Then turn around in your seat," she said.

"Something hit me on the back of the neck." Stewy looked suspiciously at Otis, who was chewing the end of his pencil and staring at the ceiling as if he were thinking hard.

"Never mind, Stewart. Go on with your work." Mrs. Gitler also glanced at Otis, before she returned to the attendance report she was working on.

That was pretty good, thought Otis, as he tore off a margin of his arithmetic workbook and chewed it into a wet ball. Then he looked around for a target.

Across the aisle he saw Ellen working feverishly on her problems. Otis knew Ellen always had trouble with arithmetic and now he watched her counting on her fingers under her desk. She wrote an answer, erased it, counted on her fingers again, and wrote another answer. Then she tugged at a lock of hair to make it grow faster. Otis could not see why Ellen was so anxious to have pigtails. What was the good of a bunch of hair flapping around all the time, anyway?

As Ellen turned a page, Otis took aim and hit her square on the cheek. Ellen gasped, and put her hand to the spot just the way he had expected her to. She, too, looked at Otis.

"Ellen," said Mrs. Gitler.

"Somebody hit me on the face with a spitball," Ellen complained.

"Otis, did you hit Ellen with a spitball?" Mrs. Gitler demanded.

"Who, me?" Otis asked.

"Otis, you are not co-operating," said Mrs. Gitler. "Let me see your arithmetic."

This was just what Otis was waiting for. Now

the class would see the look of astonishment on Mrs. Gitler's face as he handed her the sheet of completed problems.

Mrs. Gitler took his paper, glanced at it, and put it on the corner of her desk. "You may get a library book to read until the others finish," she said, as she returned to the attendance report.

How do you like that? thought Otis. He almost felt as if Mrs. Gitler was not playing fair.

He was even more disappointed when he hit Austine on the back of the neck with a ball of wet paper. All she did was turn around and stick her tongue out at him. There must be some way to make spitballs interesting. With a juicy wad in his hand, Otis looked around the room. He watched Linda Mulford walk to the teacher's desk for help on her problems. Linda was always going to Mrs. Gitler for help. As he watched Mrs. Gitler talking to Linda, an idea came to him. Boy, oh, boy, he thought, this really ought to make something happen.

Closing one eye, Otis carefully aimed at a spot one inch from Mrs. Gitler's left ear. Then he let the soggy wad fly. It whizzed through the air exactly the way he wanted it to, skimming close to Mrs. Gitler's ear without actually touching it and hitting the blackboard with a *splop.*

There! thought Otis. That ought to get results.

It did. Mrs. Gitler put down her pencil and looked at the class. Then she turned and looked at the wet spot on the blackboard. She looked at the class again and waited for complete quiet before she spoke. "Otis, you have been disturbing this class all morning."

"Who, me?" asked Otis innocently.

"Yes, you," answered Mrs. Gitler shortly. "Otis Spofford, if you throw one more spitball, I'll do something that will make you wish you'd never thought of spitballs." Then she turned back to Linda and her problems.

Otis stared at her in surprise.

"I guess you better look out," said Stewy.

"Aw, be quiet," answered Otis. Something had gone wrong. This was not what he expected. Mrs. Gitler was supposed to tell him to sit on a chair by her desk where she could keep her eye on him. She wasn't supposed to leave him wondering what she would do if he threw another spitball.

And Otis did wonder. So did the rest of the class.

"What do you suppose she'll do?" George whispered.

"I bet it's something awful," said Ellen.

Otis thought and thought. He fingered a piece of paper and tried to think what Mrs. Gitler could do to make him wish he had never thought of spitballs. He was so busy thinking that he forgot to be troublesome.

What could Mrs. Gitler mean? Would she send him to the principal's office? No, that couldn't be it. Boys were usually sent to the office for tripping people or fighting in the halls and, anyway, nothing very bad happened there. The principal just talked to you. Otis knew. He had been there several times.

Maybe Mrs. Gitler would send a note home to his mother. Otis considered this possibility but decided against it. Because spitballs didn't really do any damage, he did not think Mrs. Gitler would ask his mother to come to school, the way she had the time he discovered he could make smoke by rubbing his ruler hard and fast against the edge of his desk. This had been hard on both the ruler and the desk, which, as Mrs. Gitler explained, did not belong to Otis but to the taxpayers of the State of Oregon.

The class finished the arithmetic lesson and turned to their readers. Still Otis wondered. He hardly listened to the boys and girls reciting from the *From Here to There* reader. Without really thinking, he tore off a piece of paper and rolled it with his fingers.

"Go on," urged Stewy. "Make a spitball."

Otis looked at the paper. There was only one way to find out what Mrs. Gitler would do.

"You'll be sor-ree," warned Tommy.

Austine was watching. "Scaredy cat," she wrote on a piece of paper and held it where Otis could see it.

Otis ignored her. He looked at Mrs. Gitler, who was writing on the blackboard a list of words hard to remember. *"Though, through, thought,"* she wrote.

Otis rolled the paper into a smaller and smaller ball. Finally, just before it was time for the noon bell, he could stand it no longer. He had to find out. Quickly he put the ball of paper in his mouth. Then, as everyone in the room but Mrs. Gitler watched, he carefully aimed at a spot one inch from her right ear. Just as the bell rang, the spitball whizzed through the air and smacked against the blackboard.

Without saying a word, Mrs. Gitler opened the door into the hall. Otis was baffled. He was sure she had seen the spitball. It wasn't like Mrs. Gitler to say she would do something and then not do it.

"But, Mrs. Gitler," said Linda, when nearly everyone had left the room, "Otis threw a spitball."

"I know he did, Linda," she answered.

"But you said you would do something to him if he threw another spitball."

"Yes, Linda, but never mind about it now." Mrs. Gitler smiled at Linda. Then she smiled at Otis.

Otis began to be uneasy.

In the cafeteria, some of the boys who had left the room ahead of him dropped out of the line at the food counter to gather around Otis. "What did she do?" they wanted to know.

"She didn't do anything," Otis boasted. "She's scared to. She knows she can't make me stop throwing spitballs if I don't want to."

"That old Otis Spofford," he heard Ellen say, as she took her place in line. "Mrs. Gitler lets him do anything he wants to."

"It isn't fair," agreed Austine. "He's so awful and I think she likes him better than anybody in the room."

Otis was not so sure. There was something funny about the way Mrs. Gitler had smiled at him. Maybe he really was going to get his comeuppance.

When the class returned to their seats after lunch, Mrs. Gitler said quietly, "Otis, I want you to do something for me."

"Yes, Mrs. Gitler," said Otis, thinking she had forgotten about the spitball and wanted him to clap erasers or run an errand for her.

Mrs. Gitler said, "I want you to throw spitballs for me."

The class gasped. Throw spitballs! Whoever heard of a teacher asking someone to throw spitballs?

Even Otis was startled. He didn't know what to think, but he wasn't going to let anyone know he was taken off guard. "Sure," he said. "Any special place you want me to throw them?"

"Into the wastebasket," answered Mrs. Gitler. "I want you to sit on a chair and throw spitballs into the basket."

Otis grinned. The idea of sitting in front of the class to shoot spitballs into the wastebasket pleased him.

But Mrs. Gitler said, "Take your paper, the chair, and the basket to the back of the room."

Otis took his time about moving the chair and the wastebasket.

"Quickly, Otis," said the teacher.

"Spitball Spofford," whispered Stewy.

Otis settled himself on the chair and tore off a piece of paper. After chewing it, he threw it into the wastebasket with enough force to make a noise. He was pleased when the whole class turned around to look at him.

"All right, people. There is no need to watch Otis. We all know what he looks like," said Mrs. Gitler, as she took her pitch pipe out of her desk and the class got out its music books.

Otis chewed and threw. At first, the boys and girls peeked over their shoulders at him, but Mrs. Gitler started the singing lesson with a song about a barnyard. The class had so much fun imitating the sounds of different animals that they all lost interest in Otis.

"Moo-moo," went the first row, taking the part

of cows. The second row, who took the part of chickens, made such funny cackles that the whole class laughed and Mrs. Gitler had to start the song again.

Otis chewed more and more slowly. His mouth was dry and he began to feel lonesome all by himself at the back of the room. He stopped making spitballs altogether and sat looking out of the window. It had been raining, and drops of sparkling water dripped from the trees. How good they looked!

"Go on with your spitballs, Otis," Mrs. Gitler reminded him at the end of the song. Then she started the class on *Row, Row, Row,* which was one of their favorites.

Otis tore off another piece of paper. He took his time rolling it, because he did not feel much like making a spitball. He put it in his mouth and chewed very, very slowly. He tried counting to ten between each chew. His mouth felt drier and drier, and he decided he hated the taste of paper.

"Row, row, row your boat," sang the class.

Otis sighed. He did not want to give up and admit to Mrs. Gitler that he had had enough of spitballs. Not in front of the whole class.

"Gently down the stream," sang the class.

Gently down the stream, thought Otis. Why did everything have to make him think of water? Doggedly he kept at his spitballs, but he worked as slowly as he could. He was wondering how he

could make his spit last until school was out. He
ran his tongue around his mouth. Then he stuck
it out as far as he could to see if it were swelling
up and turning black. He could barely see the tip,
which was still pink. That was a good sign. Maybe
he could hold out.

"Merrily, merrily, merrily," trilled the class.

Suddenly the fire-drill bell rang. He was saved!
Otis leaped from his chair and was first in line at
the door. If only he could get to a drinking fountain, he knew he could make his spit last until
school was out.

"Quickly, children," said Mrs. Gitler. "Get in
line. Don't push, George. Come along, Austine."

As soon as the class was lined up two by two,
Mrs. Gitler opened the door and marched the
boys and girls rapidly through the hall and down
the stairs. She walked beside Otis, who looked
longingly at the drinking fountain as they passed.
With Mrs. Gitler beside him, there was no way he

could get to it. The more he thought about that drinking fountain, the drier his mouth felt. If he could just turn the handle and let the cool water flow into his mouth for one instant!

Outdoors, the air was cool and damp. Otis opened his mouth and drew in gasps of cool air. He didn't care if he looked like a goldfish.

"Spitball Spofford," the boys and girls whispered to him as he opened his mouth toward the sky in case it should begin to rain again.

When everyone was out of the building, the bell rang again. "All right, class, about face," ordered Mrs. Gitler.

The class turned. This left Otis and his partner at the end of the line instead of the beginning. Now it would be easier to get to the drinking fountain. As soon as the class reached the top of the stairs, Otis bent over so Mrs. Gitler would not see him and darted behind the line of boys and girls to the fountain. He turned the handle, and just as the stream of water rose almost to his mouth, he felt a hand on his shoulder. It was the principal. "You know that no one is supposed to leave his line during fire drill," said Mr. Howe, and steered Otis back to his place in line.

If that isn't my luck, thought Otis. Now my spit will never last.

As the class entered the room again, Otis was tempted to go back to his seat and hope Mrs. Gitler would forget the whole thing. But he knew that if he did Stewy or Linda or someone else would probably remind her. Anyway, he was not going to give in until he had to. He returned to his chair at the back of the room and tore off another piece of paper. Mrs. Gitler ignored him. Slowly he chewed the spitball and pitched it into the wastebasket. He tore off another piece of paper and looked at the clock. Another hour to chew and throw. A long, long hour. A minute clicked by and after a long time, another.

Otis put the paper in his mouth but he did not chew it. He just held it there a minute and took it out again. He never wanted to taste paper again. Mrs. Gitler had won. He only hoped she would not find it out.

The teacher looked up from her desk. "Well, Otis?" she asked.

Otis tried to lick his lips, but his mouth was too dry. "I guess . . . I guess . . . I've run out of spit," he said.

"Are you sure you're through throwing spitballs?" Mrs. Gitler wanted to know.

Otis did not want to answer the question, but he had to. "Yes," he said in a small voice.

"You may go out and get a drink before you return to your seat." Mrs. Gitler's eyes twinkled and she looked as if she wanted to laugh.

Otis managed a sheepish halfway grin as he went out of the room. Then he ran down the hall to the drinking fountain. How wonderful the jet of cold water looked! He drank in great gulps, stopped to gasp for breath, and gulped some more. Never had anything tasted so good. Otis drank for a long time before he wiped his mouth on his sleeve. He drank for such a long time that Mrs. Gitler came out into the hall to see what had happened to him.

"Was making me throw spitballs my come-uppance?" Otis wanted to know.

Mrs. Gitler laughed. "It would be for some boys, but I'm not sure about you." Then she shook her head. "Otis, if only you would work as hard on your spelling as you do on mischief!"

"Aw . . ." muttered Otis, because he couldn't think of anything else to say.

Back at his desk, Otis found the class was no longer interested in what he had done. As far as they were concerned, the excitement was over. He also discovered that although he was no longer thirsty, he still had a funny taste in his mouth from chewing so much paper. As he worked at his spelling, it began to bother him more and more. He wished he had something to eat that would take away the awful papery taste.

He fished through his pockets to see what he could find. Maybe he had an old stick of gum or something. In among his rabbit's foot, yo-yo, and rubber bands, Otis's fingers found the bud of garlic. He untangled it and looked at it. He wondered what it would taste like. He smelled it and decided it smelled bad and good at the same time. Holding it under his desk, he pulled off a section and peeled off the pinkish outside skin. He popped it into his mouth, bit, and for a terrible instant was sorry. Tears came to his eyes, his nose tingled, and he blew the air out of his mouth.

Instantly everyone sitting near him turned to look at him. Ellen wrinkled her nose. Austine held hers.

"Wow!" whispered Stewy. "What's that awful smell?"

Wow is right, thought Otis, as he gulped and blew again. He bit into the garlic once more. The second bite was not quite so bad as the first. Almost, but not quite. Trying to look as if he ate raw garlic all the time, he chewed a couple of times and blew again.

"Otis Spofford," Ellen said in a fierce whisper, "you stop that!"

Otis grinned. This was just what he wanted. Things were back to normal. He took a deep breath and blew as hard as he could at Ellen.

CHAPTER THREE

Otis's Scientific Experiment

ONE Monday morning when Otis went into Room Eleven, he saw an excited group of boys and girls crowded around the ledge under the windows. I wonder what they're looking at, he thought, and climbed up on a desk so he could see over their heads.

He saw two small wire cages. In each cage was a white mouse. Well! Mice in the schoolroom, thought Otis. They should be good for some excitement. Otis liked animals, but Mrs. Brewster, the manager of the apartment house where he lived, did not allow dogs or cats. Until now he had not thought of a pet mouse.

Mrs. Gitler came into the room. "Otis, you know good citizens don't stand on desks," she said, and Otis jumped down.

The whole class began to ask questions. "What are the mice doing here?" "Do we get to keep them?"

Mrs. Gitler smiled. "Take your seats, boys and girls, and I'll explain. They are not white mice. They are baby white rats. Our room is going to perform a scientific experiment."

The class was impressed. "Scientific experiment" sounded important, especially if it meant they could have rats in the schoolroom. And baby rats were much more interesting than grown-up white mice.

Mrs. Gitler went on. "This week we are going to talk about good food. These two baby rats are exactly the same weight. Each weighs forty grams.

We are going to feed one of them the same food we eat for lunch in the cafeteria. The other we will feed white bread and soda pop. We will weigh them once a week for three weeks to see which one grows faster."

The class liked this plan. Otis thought it would be fun, too, even though he knew how the experiment would turn out. Mrs. Gitler would never do anything to prove that the baby rats should drink soda pop. She would be on the side of milk and vegetables and that whole-wheat bread they always had in the cafeteria.

Ellen raised her hand. "May we name the rats?"

"That is an excellent idea," said Mrs. Gitler.

"Are they boy rats or girl rats?" someone wanted to know.

"Boy rats," said Mrs. Gitler. "They are twin brothers."

Stewy raised his hand. "We could name one rat Otis."

Everyone laughed loudly at this except Otis, who made a face at Stewy.

Then Patsy suggested Pinky, because the rats had pink ears and tails, Although some of the boys objected, the girls all agreed that Pinky was a good name.

Otis, who thought Pinky was a sissy name for a boy rat, waved his hand. "I think Mutt is a good name for the rat that gets the soda pop."

"Me, too," said George, and the others agreed.

Mrs. Gitler smiled. "It looks as if the soda-pop rat is named Mutt."

Otis looked at Mutt and almost felt as if the little rat belonged to him, because he had named him. He watched Mutt sniff around his cage. Sometimes Mutt stopped to scratch himself with his front paw. Once he scratched with his hind paw like a dog. After a while he settled into a corner of his cage. He put his head down, wrapped his hairless pink tail around his body, and went to sleep.

All morning Otis thought about the rats and wondered how he could use them to stir up some excitement. After lunch the class gathered around the ledge to watch the rat monitors lift the wire cages and set down dishes of food from the cafeteria for the two little animals. Pinky was served tiny bits of macaroni and cheese, green beans, carrot and raisin salad, whole-wheat bread, and raspberry jello. Pinky also had a few spoonfuls of milk. Mutt had a whole saucer of soda pop and half a slice of white bread. Poor Mutt, thought Otis, as he watched the little rat lap up the pop. Bread and soda pop did not look like much lunch, even for a rat.

After school Otis lingered by the rats' cages instead of trying to be the first one out of the classroom. He had several ideas for stirring up excitement, but there was something wrong with every one of them. Let the rats out of their cages? No. Mutt might get lost or stepped on. Switch cages? Too easy for Mrs. Gitler to guess. Hide one of the rats in Mrs. Gitler's desk? She was not the kind of teacher to scream at the sight of a rat. Hide a rat in Ellen's raincoat pocket? Well, that might do if he couldn't think of anything better. It was the sort of thing any boy might think of. Otis wanted to do something unusual.

By Thursday the children could see that Pinky was already larger than Mutt. His eyes were bright and his fur was glossy. Mutt spent most of his time in the corner of his cage, looking cross. The class could hardly wait until Monday, when Mrs. Gitler would weigh the rats.

When Monday came she took Pinky out of his

cage and set him on the scale. He weighed ninety grams, more than twice what he had weighed a week before. Mutt weighed forty-six grams. He had gained scarcely at all. Room Eleven was proud when Miss Joyce brought her class in to see the scientific experiment.

A whole week had gone by. I can't waste any more time, Otis said to himself. Now I've got to think of something. And that day he did.

At noon, when Otis took his place in the hot-food line in the cafeteria, he noticed everyone making faces. When he looked at the steam table to see what they were having for lunch, Otis not only made a face, he groaned and held his nose. They were having scalloped potatoes with some kind of meat, Swiss chard, sliced beets, and rice pudding. And, of course, milk and whole-wheat bread.

"Of all the awful lunches," complained George, who was standing behind Otis.

"It sure is," agreed Otis. "I don't see why we can't have hot dogs and ice cream every day." He gloomily handed the cashier his money. Twenty perfectly good cents wasted, he thought, as he carried his tray to a table. Scalloped potatoes and Swiss chard! Otis carefully picked the meat out of his potatoes and ate that first.

"I'm sure glad I brought my lunch," said Tommy, who was sitting across from Otis, eating the centers out of his sandwiches.

"You're lucky," agreed Otis, poking at his Swiss chard. "I don't see why this stuff would even be good for a rat."

Hey, wait a minute, Otis suddenly thought. He was about to have an idea. He could feel it coming on. This might be very good food for a rat. If he gave Mutt good food, without anybody's seeing him, Mutt might outgrow Pinky. That would really fix the experiment, because everybody would think it was white bread and soda pop that had made Mutt grow. He could just see Mrs. Gitler's face. And boy, oh, boy, the cafeteria would have to start serving soda pop! That was the best part of all. Soda pop in the cafeteria!

Otis was so pleased with his inspiration that he ate his beets and Swiss chard without even thinking about them. It was a perfect idea. Difficult, of course, but worth it. Already he could see cases of orange and pink and green soda pop stacked in the cafeteria. Now all he had to do was figure out what to feed Mutt and how to slip the food to him without being seen.

That evening Otis went into the kitchen, where his mother was preparing dinner. She was in a hurry, because she had got home late from the Spofford School of the Dance. Otis watched her drop a slab of frozen peas into boiling water and put two frozen cubed steaks into a frying pan. "I'm hungry," he said. "We had an awful lunch at school today."

The peas boiled over onto the stove. "Run along, dear, and don't bother me," said Mrs. Spofford, wiping up the stove. "Mother has been teaching tap dancing all afternoon and she's tired."

Otis leaned against the refrigerator. "Say, Mom, isn't there something that's better for people to eat than scalloped potatoes?"

Mrs. Spofford forked two potatoes baking in the oven. "Why, almost anything, I suppose. Milk and cheese and—oh, I don't know. Lots of things."

Cheese! Of course! Rats liked cheese. He should have thought of that himself. Otis helped himself to a piece of cheese from the refrigerator. Then he noticed a bottle of vitamin pills on the drain board. "Say, Mom, can I have some vitamins?" he asked.

"Yes, dear. Now please run along," said Mrs. Spofford, as she turned the flame down under the meat.

Otis added a handful of vitamin pills to the

piece of cheese in his pocket. Cheese and vitamins. They ought to make Mutt grow. Now all he had to do was to find a way to slip them into Mutt's cage without being seen. That was the hardest part of his plan.

When Otis arrived at school early the next morning, he found the door of Room Eleven locked. In a few minutes Mrs. Gitler appeared with the key in her hand. "Good morning, Otis," she said. "My, aren't you bright and early?"

"I . . . uh . . . thought I'd come early and study my spelling," Otis explained. If only Mrs. Gitler would unlock the door and go away.

"Splendid," said Mrs. Gitler, giving Otis a surprised look. Or was it a suspicious look? Otis couldn't tell.

When Mrs. Gitler was busy writing some arithmetic problems on the blackboard, Otis left his desk and went to the rats' cages. Mutt was huddled miserably in a corner. Otis put his hand in his pocket and broke off a piece of cheese.

"Otis," said Mrs. Gitler, without even turning around to look at him, "if you aren't going to study your spelling, you must go out on the playground until the bell rings."

Otis took his seat. He had said he had come early to study spelling, so he supposed he had to sit there with a book in front of him.

All morning Otis waited for a chance to slip food into Mutt's cage. By lunch period he was forced to form another plan. He went into the cloakroom and pretended he could not find his sweater. Then he waited quietly until all the other boys and girls left the room. He heard Mrs. Gitler shut the door. Then he heard something he did not expect. The key turned in the lock. Otis was locked in.

As long as the door was locked, he did not have

to worry about being discovered. That was something. Stooping, so he could not be seen through the windows, Otis hurried to the rats. When he lifted Mutt's cage and put down a piece of cheese and a vitamin pill, the little rat scurried over to the food and nibbled greedily.

Good old Mutt. He must have been awfully hungry. The trouble was, Mutt wasn't the only one who was hungry. Otis was hungry too. He wondered what the others were eating in the cafeteria. Maybe it was hot-dog day. Otis watched Mutt finish the cheese and gnaw the vitamin pill, which slipped away from him until he learned to hold it with his paws. Otis was so hungry that he took the rest of the cheese out of his pocket. It was covered with fuzz, but he didn't care. He gave Mutt another piece and ate the rest himself. When it was time for the bell to ring again, Otis made sure there were no telltale crumbs in the cage before he hid in the cloakroom once more.

"Where were you?" Stewy asked, when Mrs. Gitler unlocked the door and the class streamed into the room. "I didn't see you in the cafeteria."

"Oh, around," said Otis vaguely, as he joined the group watching the monitors feed the rats. So it really had been hot-dog day in the cafeteria! Watching Pinky nibble a piece of hot dog made Otis hungrier than ever.

"Mutt isn't eating his bread," someone said. "Do you suppose he's sick?"

"He's probably just tired of it," said Ellen. "You'd get tired of it too, if that's all you had to eat." Then she added, "Poor little Mutt."

The next day Otis brought more cheese and another vitamin pill to Mutt. He also brought a sandwich and a cupcake for himself, so he and the rat ate lunch together. Otis thought Mutt had grown a little already. If only he could keep on feeding him without being caught!

The third day, Otis decided not to feed the rat

at noon. Stewy had asked too many questions about why he wasn't in the cafeteria.

"I think Mutt's growing," Otis heard someone say.

"So do I. His stomach sticks out," Tommy said. "And he's frisky, too. Look at him."

Otis was delighted with the way his private experiment was turning out. Just wait till Mrs. Gitler weighed Mutt. When he asked her if she didn't think the cafeteria should serve soda pop, she wouldn't have a thing to say against it.

As he was leaving the room for recess, Otis made a detour past the cages in the hope that he could slip Mutt's food to him. Stewy followed close at his heels. "What are you tagging around after me for?" Otis asked.

"I'm just looking at the rats," said Stewy. "What would I tag after you for?"

Otis decided he had better be quiet. He did not want to make Stewy suspicious.

When Otis had no better luck feeding Mutt at lunch time, he began to be uneasy. What if he couldn't get any food to Mutt? Maybe the rat would lose weight and he would have to start his experiment all over again.

Finally, as the class left the room to go to the auditorium for folk dancing, Otis managed to slip Mutt's food into the cage. Then he worried all during folk dancing. What if Mutt didn't eat it all up while the class was out of the room? But when they returned, Otis was relieved to find every crumb gone.

Friday was worst of all. Otis scarcely had time for breakfast, he was so anxious to get to school early. The door of Room Eleven was locked as usual, and there was no opportunity to slip food into the cage during the morning. By lunch time Otis was desperate. Even though he had not brought a sandwich for himself, he hid in the cloakroom again and took a chance that Stewy would not miss him. When the classroom door was safely locked, he watched Mutt gobble the cheese he had brought him and look around for more. Hungry as he was, Otis gave the rat the rest of the cheese and a vitamin pill.

Suddenly Otis heard the sound of a key in the door. Mrs. Gitler was coming back! He looked frantically for a place to hide and made it to the cloakroom just as the classroom door opened. He crouched halfway between the cloakroom's two doors. Just to be safe, he pulled someone's raincoat over him. He heard Mrs. Gitler lock the classroom door from the inside. Then he heard her walk across the room, humming to herself.

Otis was afraid to move. He was almost afraid to breathe. Was she going to stay in the room for the whole lunch hour, for Pete's sake? He heard the drawer of her desk open. More humming. Then a snapping noise. What could that be? A compact, of course. Mrs. Gitler was powdering her nose.

Otis's left leg went to sleep. The drawer closed. A chair scraped. Mrs. Gitler walked down the side of the room by the windows. Would she . . . ? Yes, she did. She stopped by the rats' cages.

Otis's right leg went to sleep. If only he could be sure Mutt had finished the vitamin pill! He tried wiggling his toes inside his shoes to ease the numbness in his legs. Just then Mrs. Gitler started to walk toward the back of the room. Otis held his breath. He didn't know what he would do if she came into the cloakroom. He heard her pause at one of the cloakroom doors. Then she passed it. He was able to breathe again as he heard her open a cupboard, take something out, and close it again. If only she would leave the room!

Otis's hungry stomach began to rumble and

then to growl. Frantically he pressed his arms against his middle. His stomach made an interesting gurgling noise. He squirmed silently. His stomach growled back at him. Surely it was loud enough for Mrs. Gitler to hear.

Mrs. Gitler's footsteps returned to the front of the room and Otis heard her sit down at her desk. He heard papers rustling and decided she was settled for the rest of the lunch period. At least she couldn't hear his noisy stomach from the front of the room.

Why did I ever think this was such a good idea anyway, thought Otis miserably. Maybe it wasn't such a good joke after all. Maybe the joke was really on him. Then he thought how close he was to rat-weighing time. No, he wouldn't give up. He would hang on a little longer. His legs felt as if they were stuck full of pins. Grimly he listened for each minute to click by on the electric clock.

Each minute seemed so long he was sure the clock had stopped. Outside he heard the children laughing and shouting. He wondered if anyone missed him.

Finally, when Otis was sure he could not remain motionless another instant, the first bell rang and Mrs. Gitler unlocked the door. He waited until the halls were filled with noise before he came out from under the raincoat. Then he clung to a coat hook with one hand while he tried to make his stiff, prickly legs work.

Stewy was first into the cloakroom. He was eating a chocolate bar filled with almonds.

Otis had to swallow before he could say, "Hi."

"What are you doing here?" demanded Stewy suspiciously.

"I stayed in. I don't feel so good," said Otis, looking hungrily at the chocolate bar. And it was true. He couldn't think of a time when he had felt worse.

Stewy hung up his jacket, popped the rest of the chocolate into his mouth, and licked his fingers.

By that time Otis's feet were working once more and were able to carry him into the classroom. As he walked past the rats' cages he saw that the vitamin pill had disappeared, but he wondered uneasily what Mrs. Gitler had seen. He was glad his experiment was nearly at an end. He couldn't keep it up any longer. Not even for soda pop in the cafeteria.

When Monday morning finally arrived, Otis shoved his way through the excited boys and girls crowded around the rats. Sure enough, Mutt was bigger. Otis put his finger against the cage. With his whiskers quivering, Mutt put his front paws up on the wire and sniffed at Otis's finger. Good old Mutt, thought Otis. He knows me. He's just like my very own pet rat.

And then Otis began to wonder. What was go-

ing to happen to the rats when the experiment ended? Mutt was the only pet he had ever had. He was going to miss him when he was gone, unless . . . Maybe there was some way he could get to take Mutt home with him. Mrs. Brewster would not have to know about a pet rat, and Otis's mother was too busy to care.

Otis went to the teacher's desk. "Mrs. Gitler, what will happen to the rats when the experiment ends?" he asked.

"We'll talk about that when the time comes," she answered, and went on working on her lesson plans.

That only made Otis more anxious. After the

class had taken their seats, he couldn't keep from watching Mutt. Such a fine healthy rat! And all because he had worked to make sure that he had good food. Otis had to find some way to keep him.

As Mrs. Gitler took the scales out of the cupboard, Otis still had not thought of a plan. He wished she would hurry as he watched her adjust the weights and set Pinky on the scale. She slid the weights back and forth some more before she said, "Pinky weighs one hundred and thirty grams." Then she lifted Mutt out of his cage, weighed him, and announced, "Mutt weighs one hundred and thirty-seven grams!"

Mutt was bigger than Pinky! Everyone began to talk at once.

"I have only one pair of ears," said Mrs. Gitler. "I can hear only one person at a time."

Secretly Otis felt that he had Mrs. Gitler in a pretty tight spot. He raised his hand and asked, "If Mutt grew more on white bread and soda pop than Pinky did on school lunches, doesn't that mean we should drink soda pop and eat white bread in the cafeteria?"

Soda pop in the cafeteria! Everyone had something to say.

Mrs. Gitler looked stern until the room was silent. Then she spoke quietly. "No, Otis, it does not mean that we should eat white bread and drink soda pop in the cafeteria." She paused to look sadly at the class. "It means that some boy or girl in this room has spoiled our experiment by feeding Mutt."

Otis stared at his teacher. Leave it to Mrs. Gitler to guess what had happened. Much as he disliked admitting it, even to himself, he had to admire her. You couldn't put anything over on Mrs. Gitler. At least, not very often. Otis squirmed uncomfortably. Poor Mrs. Gitler. How disappointed she looked—to think that one of her boys or girls would spoil the scientific experiment.

Now Otis did not know what to do. He had expected Mrs. Gitler to be surprised or maybe cross, not to look sad and disappointed. While Mrs. Gitler looked sadly at the class, Otis made up his mind to tell her what he had done. He would say he was sorry, and when Mrs. Gitler forgave him he would ask for Mutt.

But before he could get the words out, Ellen spoke. "Mrs. Gitler, I . . . I . . ." She gulped. Otis thought she sounded as if she was about to cry. "I fed Mutt. He . . . he looked so little and hungry that I felt sorry for him." She gulped again and looked miserably at Mrs. Gitler.

Otis stared at Ellen. Mrs. Gitler surprised him, but Ellen astounded him. Old Ellen Tebbits saying she fed Mutt just when he was going to tell what he had done. Well, he didn't believe it. It wasn't true. She couldn't have fed Mutt. Look at all the trouble he had had, trying to slip cheese and vitamin pills to him.

"How could you feed him without anybody seeing you?" Otis demanded.

"Yes, Ellen, and tell us what you fed him," said Mrs. Gitler.

"Every day I wrapped some of my lunch from the cafeteria in a paper napkin." Ellen paused to sniff unhappily. "And then I waited till everyone had gone home and then I asked the janitor to let me into the room for a minute. I didn't mean to spoil the experiment. Mutt just looked so . . . so hungry." Ellen burst into tears.

Now why didn't I think of that? thought Otis. That Ellen! He couldn't help feeling sorry for her, she looked so unhappy, but just the same . . . Mutt was his rat.

There was an embarrassed silence until Mrs. Gitler said briskly, "Even if the experiment didn't turn out as we planned, I'm sure we have all learned the important thing. That is, we must eat good food if we are to grow and be healthy."

That isn't what I learned, thought Otis. I learned you've got to be careful or some girl will get ahead of you.

Austine raised her hand. "Mrs. Gitler, if we aren't going on with the experiment, what is going to happen to Mutt and Pinky?"

"We'll find good homes for them," Mrs. Gitler answered. "Is there anyone who would like a pet rat?"

Otis waved his hand wildly, but Mrs. Gitler did not see him. She asked, "Who would like to take Pinky home?"

Otis stopped waving his hand. He wanted Mutt. The class finally decided Tommy should have Pinky. Stewy wanted him, but he already had a dog. Tommy, who had neither a dog nor a cat, could give a good home to a rat.

Now was Otis's chance. He waved his hand frantically. "Mrs. Gitler," he said. "Mrs. Gitler."

Otis knew she saw him, even though she said, "Yes, Ellen?"

Ellen twisted her handkerchief as she spoke. "I know I spoiled the experiment, but I'd like awfully much to take Mutt home. I sort of feel like he's my rat."

Otis didn't know what to do. He couldn't let Ellen have Mutt. He had to do something. "But I fed him too," he protested. "He's just as much mine as Ellen's. I went without my lunch to feed him." Otis watched Mrs. Gitler anxiously. She just had to see how important it was for him to have Mutt for his very own. He felt everyone staring at him. "Well, I did feed him," said Otis, when no one spoke. "And I gave him vitamin pills besides. He's just as much mine as he is Ellen's."

"Well, Otis, aren't you rather slow in telling us about this?" Mrs. Gitler looked stern, but Otis could see that behind her stern look she wanted to laugh.

This was no laughing matter to Otis. "I was going to tell, but Ellen beat me to it," he explained.

"Oh, I see," said Mrs. Gitler. "Yes, Ellen, since you told us about feeding Mutt first, you may have him for a pet."

"Aw, that's no fair," muttered Otis, trying to cover up his disappointment.

"What did you say, Otis?" asked Mrs. Gitler.

"Nothing." Otis scowled and slid down in his seat. That Ellen Tebbits! Taking his rat! Why, you wouldn't think a girl who was always neat and clean like Ellen would even like rats.

That afternoon Otis watched Mrs. Gitler put Mutt in a chalk box for Ellen to carry home. It seemed to him that he had never wanted anything as much as he wanted Mutt for his very own.

Well, it was too late now. He took one last look at Mutt's bright eyes and quivering whiskers before he started home.

When Otis reached the apartment house he found Bucky, a kindergarten boy who lived in the same building, sitting on the front steps waiting for him. Although Otis didn't care much about playing with a five-year-old, he couldn't help liking Bucky, because he knew the little boy admired him and wanted to be like him when he grew up.

"Hi," said Bucky, who was wearing his cowboy suit. "Let's play like we're cowboys."

Otis sat down on the steps. "Not today," he said glumly, and began to pull a piece of rubber off the sole of his sneaker. He wished there was someone around to play with besides a little kindergartner. If only he had Mutt!

Then Otis looked down the street and saw Ellen coming toward him. She had changed to her play clothes and was carrying the chalk box. She looked unhappy.

"Hi," said Otis, wondering where she was going.

"Hello, Otis." Ellen stopped in front of the steps. "My mother says she won't have a rat in the house and I have to get rid of Mutt right away. I thought I'd give him to you, because you fed him and would take good care of him." She held out the chalk box.

Otis took it and slid back the lid to look at Mutt, who was cowering in a corner. "Gee . . ." said Otis. "Gee . . . thanks, Ellen." Gently he lifted Mutt out and stroked his soft white fur. Mutt snuggled into his hand. His very own Mutt!

"Could I come and see him sometimes?" Ellen asked timidly.

"Sure, any time." Otis decided Ellen wasn't so bad after all, even if she was always neat and clean and well behaved.

As Ellen left, Bucky began to chant, "Otis has a girl. Otis has a girl."

"You keep quiet," said Otis fiercely, "or I'll . . . I'll . . ."

"If you do anything to me, I'll tell the management on you," said Bucky.

"Well, keep quiet or I won't let you play with my rat," said Otis.

Bucky kept quiet.

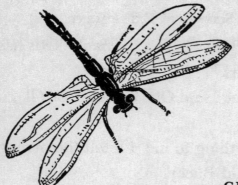

CHAPTER FOUR

Otis and the Thirty Bugs

I WISH I could stir up a little excitement around here, thought Otis, one day after school. His mother was busy at the Spofford School of the Dance, and Mrs. Brewster said she didn't want him underfoot when she was trying to run the vacuum cleaner in the front hall of the apartment house. Otis didn't see how she could call sliding down the banisters being underfoot.

Otis wandered over to Stewy's house to see if

Stewy had any ideas. Stewy couldn't think of anything to do either, so the two boys and Stewy's dog, Spud, started aimlessly down the street.

This isn't very exciting, thought Otis, as he watched Spud stop to scratch. The dog stood on three legs while he scratched with his hind foot.

"That dog doesn't know enough to sit down to scratch," observed Otis, hoping to get a rise out of Stewy.

"It takes a smart dog to stand up to scratch," boasted Stewy. "Let's go over to the high school and watch football practice."

"O.K.," agreed Otis, leapfrogging over a fire hydrant. "Let's go."

Suddenly Stewy pointed. "Hey, look! Isn't that Hack Battleson over there?"

"It sure is," agreed Otis in an awed voice, as both boys stopped to admire Hack Battleson. Gee, thought Otis, I wish I had a piece of paper. Maybe he would give me his autograph.

Hack was not only fullback and captain of the Zachary P. Taylor High School football team, he had also been chosen the most promising football player in the whole city by the sports editor of the *Oregonian*. Sometimes he was called Five-yard Battleson, because whenever his team needed to gain one yard, Hack could gain five.

Otis and Stewy often watched Hack at football practice. That was one time when Otis did not want to stir up any excitement. He just wanted to watch Hack kick the football farther than anyone else on the field and tackle the dummies so hard that the dust flew out in clouds. Twice Stewy's father had taken the boys to see Hack play in a real game in the stadium on the other side of the city.

"I wonder how come he isn't out at football practice now," said Otis. Hack, who was standing on his front lawn, held a fruit jar in one hand and appeared to be looking for something.

"Sure is funny," agreed Stewy. "What's he doing anyway?"

"Search me," said Otis. "Gee, look at those muscles. I wish I had muscles like that." Otis made up his mind to start doing exercises that very night. Otis noticed that Hack stood with one thumb hooked through the belt of his jeans. Otis hooked his thumb through the belt of his jeans too.

Just then the boys saw Hack leap into the air and clap the lid on the jar. He looked into the jar, shook his head, and looked around once more.

The boys sat down on the curb opposite Hack's house to watch. "I know what," said Otis. "Let's give him a yell like we learned at the game."

The boys began to yell at the top of their voices, "T-T-T-A-Y. L-L-L-O-R. T-A-Y. L-O-R. Ta-a-ay-lor!"

Hack paid no attention. He leaped into the air with his fruit jar again. The boys got up and

walked across the street, where they stood in front of Hack's house.

"Let's try the Zachary P. Taylor football song," whispered Otis.

The boys began to sing.

> *"Z. P. Taylor, school of honored name,*
> *Fight, fight, fight along the road to fame.*
> *We'll win because of might,*
> *We'll keep your victory bright!*
> *Rah! Rah! Rah!"*

This time Hack glanced at the boys and the dog. "Hi, kids," he said, and went on hunting.

Otis and Stewy looked at each other. Hack Battleson, Five-yard Battleson, fullback and captain of the Zachary P. Taylor football team, actually had spoken to them. Encouraged, the boys moved closer.

Otis was first to get up his courage. "What are you doing?" he asked.

"Trying to catch insects," answered Hack, in a way that showed he was much too busy to waste time talking to grade-school boys.

"How come you're catching bugs when there's football practice going on?" Stewy asked.

"I have to," said Hack.

"Why?" persisted Otis.

Hack scowled. "For biology class. We were supposed to hand in a collection of thirty insects last week, and I was too busy with football practice to catch them. Now the teacher says if I don't hand them in by tomorrow, she'll tell the principal and then I can't play on the team."

"Gee, and the big game with Benjamin Harrison High is next week," said Otis. He and Stewy were shocked. To think that a teacher could not only give orders to Hack Battleson but could make him miss football practice!

Otis recovered first. "I'll catch them for you, Hack," he said eagerly. It wasn't every boy who had the chance to do something for the captain of the team and the best football player in the whole city.

"Would you?" Hack's manner toward the younger boys suddenly changed. "Say, that would be swell! Then I could go back to football practice."

"I'll catch them too," said Stewy.

"You keep out of this. It was my idea," said Otis, who did not want any help from Stewy. He wanted to tell people that he alone caught thirty insects for Hack Battleson. Why, it was practically the same thing as saving the big game for the Zachary P. Taylor High School.

"I thought of it at the same time," objected Stewy. "You just *said* it first."

"That's what counts," said Otis. "Why don't you go exercise your dog or something?"

"He doesn't need exercise," answered Stewy.

"Then is it O.K. if I catch them for you?" Otis asked Hack. He was anxious to have it clearly understood that he was the one to collect the insects.

"I don't care who catches them," answered Hack, who was in a hurry to get to the football field. "Just so somebody has thirty insects here by six-thirty. It can't be any later, because I'll probably be up all night trying to identify them, as it is. And they all have to be insects. You can tell an insect because it has six legs. Centipedes and things like that don't count."

Otis was disappointed that Stewy was to have an equal chance, but he didn't feel that he could say anything to Hack about it.

"And they have to be in good condition," continued Hack, as he held up his fruit jar. "See that piece of cotton in the jar? It's soaked in cleaning fluid—the kind that takes spots off clothes. When I catch an insect I put it in the jar and put the lid on a minute. The fumes kill the insect without hurting it."

"Sure. I get it," said Otis. "How about letting me take your jar?"

"Hey, that's no fair," objected Stewy. "That way you'd have a head start."

"Sure I'd have a head start," said Otis.

"For Pete's sake, if you kids are going to stand there fighting all day, I'll get another jar for you," said Hack, who was really pleased to have two boys so anxious to work for him.

Otis and Stewy glared at each other until

Hack returned with the
second jar. "O.K., kids.
See you at six-thirty."
Hack waved as he hur-
ried off to the Zachary P.
Taylor football field.

"You just wait. I'll beat you to the thirty bugs,"
said Stewy.

Otis did not waste time answering. At least, he
had a head start. At home he had two insects: a
dead dragonfly he had picked up once because
he thought it was pretty, and a yellow butterfly
that had died when he tried to keep it in a jar.
Now he pawed through some dead leaves under
a shrub until he saw an earwig. He scooped it into
the jar and screwed on the lid. Stewy watched him
and then did the same thing. The boys glowered
at each other.

Otis decided he'd better get away from Stewy,
or Stewy would copy all his ideas. Otis knew he

had to work fast if he was going to catch all those insects by six-thirty. "So long," he said, and ran down the street.

Otis stopped to hunt among some flowers in a neighbor's yard. When he found a tiny green aphis clinging to the underside of a rose leaf, he carefully scooped it off and added it to the earwig in his jar. A ladybug flitted past, but before Otis could grab it, it lit on a rosebush growing on a trellis against the house. When Otis tried to catch the ladybug, it flew to a leaf just out of his reach. Otis started to climb the trellis.

The lady who lived in the house burst out onto the front porch. "Otis Spofford! You come down out of my climbing President Hoover this instant!" she ordered.

Otis was so startled that he grabbed at a thorny branch instead of the trellis. "Your what?" he asked, trying to untangle his T-shirt from the thorns.

"My climbing President Hoover. My prize rose-bush." The lady was very cross. "I won't have it broken. Come down at once."

The ladybug flitted away, so Otis jumped to the ground. Thorns ripped his T-shirt, but he couldn't let the ladybug out of sight.

"And don't you come into my garden again," said the owner of the rosebush.

"I won't," promised Otis, keeping his eye on the ladybug and thinking that if he were a grownup with a prize rosebush, he would want a boy to catch bugs in it. He jumped up and cupped his hands together. There, I got you, he thought. That was one insect closer to winning the game.

In the next yard Otis pried a rock out of a rock garden, but all he found under it was a worm and a crawly thing with too many legs to be an insect. A fly buzzed by and Otis wasted several precious minutes chasing it before it flew out of reach. He

saw a bee hovering over a flower. Quickly he
clapped it, flower and all, into his jar.

Otis was about to investigate another rock when
the owner of the garden appeared. She smiled at
Otis. "Hello, boy. Come here and let me show you
all my pretty flowers," she said.

It was perfectly plain to Otis that she didn't
really want him in her garden at all. He didn't see
why grownups had to be so fussy about a few old
flowers. "No, thank you," he said. He didn't have
time to make friends with anyone. Not today, anyway.

The lady started across the yard toward Otis.
She looked so determined to be friendly that Otis
decided he'd better leave in a hurry, or he would
be looking at pretty flowers whether he wanted
to or not. "Well . . . uh . . . good-by," he said,
and ran down the street, feeling that he had had a
narrow escape.

As Otis was passing Stewy's house, a tiny moving speck on the sidewalk caught his eye. It was an ant that Otis lost no time in scraping up with a twig and poking into his jar.

"That's my bug," yelled Stewy, from half a block away. "You give it back to me."

"It is not," Otis yelled back.

"It is, too. I saw you pick it up in front of my house." Stewy looked hot and cross.

"It was on the sidewalk, and sidewalks don't belong to you. They belong to the city." Otis wasn't going to waste time arguing. When he reached his apartment house, he found Bucky sitting on the front steps waiting for him.

"Say, Otis," said Bucky, "let's play like we're—"

"I know what," interrupted Otis. "Let's play like we're scientists hunting bugs in the jungle. Let's see how many bugs we can capture."

Bucky was delighted to receive this much attention from Otis. "Dead or alive?" he asked.

"Alive," said Otis. "We'll shut them up in this

jar. You go that way and I'll go this way." He found a spider in the shrubs and was about to put it into his jar when he remembered. A spider had eight legs. It was not an insect.

"I've got one," shrieked Bucky. "It's like a lady-bug only yellow with black dots." He held up his two hands cupped together.

"Swell," said Otis. "Here, put it in the jar."

"I can't," said Bucky. "It's a fierce jungle bug. It's putting up a terrible fight. It's trying to eat me up alive. Help, help!" Bucky fell to the tiny patch of grass in front of the apartment house, where he rolled and kicked.

"Oh, for Pete's sake." Otis was disgusted. He

might have known this was the way a kindergartner would behave. "I'll save you," he called, and fell to the grass beside Bucky to pry open his hands and take out the bug.

"You saved my life," panted Bucky. "This is a keen game."

Otis was not so sure, but at least he had another insect for Hack Battleson. Otis then caught a fly, a mosquito, and a white moth. Bucky captured a beetle, a stink bug, and a grasshopper that put up a battle and spit brown juice all over Bucky's hands.

"There's Stewy across the street," exclaimed Bucky. "Look, he's got a jar too."

"Come on, let's go around in back," suggested Otis quickly.

"Hey, Stewy," yelled Bucky. "Are you playing like you're hunting fierce bugs in the jungle too?"

"Sh-h-h," hissed Otis, too late.

Stewy came across the street. He held his jar

behind his back, so Otis could not see how many bugs he had. He glared at Otis, who also held his jar out of sight. Then he said to Bucky, "How would you like to hunt bugs in the jungle with me for a change?"

"Hey, cut it out," said Otis. "Bucky and I are having a keen time all by ourselves, aren't we, Bucky?"

Bucky beamed. "We sure are."

Otis stepped around Stewy to try to catch a glimpse of his jar. If only he knew how many insects Stewy had! Stewy saw what Otis was trying to do and moved a couple of feet so Otis couldn't see behind him.

"I know what," said Bucky. "Let's all play like we're hunting in the jungle together."

"Let's not," said Otis and Stewy together. This time Stewy tried to see behind Otis's back, while Otis glared and moved away.

"Guess I'll be going now," said Stewy. "I'm

about through anyway. So long. See you at six-thirty." Stewy started home. Then he called back, "Unless I decide to take my thirty bugs over sooner."

"I like Stewy. Don't you?" asked Bucky.

Otis did not answer. He was too busy worrying. Was Stewy telling the truth or was he bluffing? He wished he knew. Otis tried to think where Stewy might have found a lot of insects all at once. That gave him an idea. "Come on, Bucky," he said.

On either side of the front door of the apartment house was a porch light that burned all night. Otis knew that insects were attracted to them. He boosted Bucky up to one of the lights and told him how to unscrew it. He was rewarded by a shower of dust and dead moths.

Mrs. Brewster flung open the front door. She had a dish towel wrapped around her hair and a broom in her hand. "Now what are you boys up to?" she demanded, as she began to sweep the moths off the porch. "Just look at the litter on this porch."

Bucky looked frightened, but Otis could not let that collection of moths be smashed to bits by the broom. "I'll sweep the porch," he offered. "We were just cleaning the bugs out of the light for you. I'd like to sweep the porch."

"All right," said Mrs. Brewster crossly. "But see that you get it clean. Goodness knows I have enough other work to do."

That was close, thought Otis, as he got on his hands and knees to examine his harvest. There was not only an assortment of moths; there were three kinds of gnats as well. Of course, the bugs had been cooked by the heat of the light, but Otis was sure Hack wouldn't mind, because their legs and wings were all in place. He hadn't said the bugs had to be raw.

The second light produced two more moths and several insects Otis already had. If I were collecting just for fun, I could save them for traders, Otis thought, and picked a dead wasp out of a cobweb.

"Dead bugs aren't any fun," complained Bucky. "They don't put up a fight."

"Why don't you play like you're a janitor?" suggested Otis, who knew Bucky would do anything to please him. "You could have lots of fun sweeping the porch for Mrs. Brewster."

"O.K.," agreed Bucky.

Otis continued to hunt alone. Fortunately this was the day his mother gave a private ballet lesson after her tap-dancing class, so he knew she would be late getting home. He hoped Stewy's mother would insist on his taking time to eat dinner before six-thirty.

At six o'clock Otis went into his apartment, where he emptied a box of crackers onto the drain board. Then he lined the box with cotton and

arranged his insects in rows. I'll bet old Stewy won't think of this, he thought. He'll probably bring his all bunched up in the jar. Counting the dragonfly and butterfly, Otis had twenty-eight insects.

At seven minutes after six, Otis found a different kind of ant crawling on the garbage can behind the apartment house. That made twenty-nine. By a quarter after six, Otis was frantically beating the shrubs. He saw flies, earwigs, ladybugs—insects he already had. At twenty-five minutes past six, he knew he could hunt no longer. He had to take a chance on finding his last insect on the way to Hack's house.

Stewy was sitting on Hack's front steps with a candy box on his knees. Spud lay at his feet. "Hi," he said. "Hack's late getting home, or I'd have given him my thirty bugs a long time ago."

Otis pretended to admire his collection so much that he did not hear. However, he was careful to close the lid of his box before he sat down beside Stewy.

"Just remember, I was here first," said Stewy.

Otis did not say anything. Holding his box so Stewy couldn't see into it, he took out the dragonfly and held it up to admire. "Hack will be glad to get this. You don't often see such a beauty," he remarked, because he was sure Stewy did not have a dragonfly. By the worried look on Stewy's face, he knew he was right.

"He'd probably rather have my queen bee," said Stewy.

Now it was Otis's turn to look worried. Did Stewy really have a queen bee? How did he know it was a queen? Otis decided it was probably a plain old bumblebee that he just called a queen.

The boys sat in uneasy silence until Hack Battleson turned the corner. "Hi, Hack," they yelled, and then glared at each other.

"Hi, kids," answered Hack. "Sorry I'm late, but I had a few things to talk over with the coach."

Otis looked admiringly at Hack. Maybe someday he would have to talk over a few things with the coach. Maybe when he got to high school the coach would remember that he was the boy who saved the big game by catching bugs. And he would have a purple sweater with a red *T* on one side and three red stripes on the left sleeve to show he had played on the team three years, just like Hack.

"Here are the bugs," said Stewy.

Annoyed with himself for letting Stewy get ahead of him, Otis thrust his box at Hack too. "I've got some keen insects," he said.

Hack sat down on the steps. He opened Stewy's box first and counted all the insects in it while

Otis waited anxiously. "Thirty," announced Hack.

I guess that's that, thought Otis, suddenly feeling tired and hungry. He had not saved the game for the Zachary P. Taylor High School after all. He had lost it by one bug. Just one little old bug. And Stewy would never let him forget it, either.

Hack opened Otis's box. "Look at that dragonfly," he said. "That's a beauty."

Otis felt a little better. At least Hack Battleson admired his dragonfly. That was something. Otis stepped over Spud and sat down on the steps while Hack counted his insects. "Twenty-nine," said Hack. "You're one short."

"Ha!" said Stewy. "So you didn't have thirty at all."

You needn't rub it in, thought Otis, as his eye fell on Stewy's collection. "Hey, wait a minute!" he shouted. "Neither do you. You've got a spider and they don't count. They've got eight legs."

"That's right," agreed Hack. "If they have eight

legs, they aren't insects. Let's have another look at that box."

Surely Hack would take Otis's collection now because of the dragonfly. Otis waited anxiously. Spud stood up on three legs to scratch. As Otis watched the dog, he was suddenly stunned by an idea. If only Stewy didn't think of it at the same time! Otis quickly looked over Stewy's collection. No, Stewy didn't have one. That made his idea even better.

But Stewy had an idea of his own. "I know what," Otis heard him say to Hack. "I'll pull off a couple of its legs. Then it will be a six-legged bug."

Otis parted Spud's coarse hair and began to search for something.

"That wouldn't work," objected Hack, to Stewy's suggestion.

Otis's thumb and forefinger closed on something which he quickly popped into the jar.

"I don't see why," Stewy was saying. "I bet the teacher would think it was some new kind of bug."

"She's too smart for that," said Hack. "Somebody tried it already."

Then Otis spoke. "Here's my thirtieth insect," he said, as he reached into the jar.

"What is it?" asked Hack.

"A flea," answered Otis.

"A flea!" Hack began to laugh, but he took the tiny insect and added it to Otis's collection. Then he closed the box. "Thanks a lot," he said. "I guess I ought to get a pretty good grade on this collection, even if I am late handing it in."

Stewy turned to Otis. "Where did you get that flea?" he demanded.

"Off Spud," said Otis.

"That's what I thought." Stewy was angry. "That was my flea! You took my flea."

"Don't you wish you'd thought of it?" jeered Otis. "So long, Hack."

"Spud's fleas are my fleas and you didn't have any right to take it," said Stewy, as Hack went

into the house. "It was just plain cheating, that's what it was."

"Aw, you're just mad because you weren't smart enough to think of it first," taunted Otis.

"Otis Spofford, I'll . . . I'll . . ." Stewy sputtered.

"You'll have to catch me first," yelled Otis, and ran down the street. And as he ran he was no longer Otis Spofford running home to dinner. He was Five-yard Spofford, running ninety-nine and a half yards for a touchdown to save the big game for the Zachary P. Taylor High School.

CHAPTER FIVE

Otis, the Unfriendly Indian

ONE Friday morning Otis left his apartment house a little bit late for school, as usual. The first snow of the year had fallen during the night. The bite of frosty air on his cheeks and the sight of his neighborhood so changed by the blanket of snow made Otis feel that something exciting was going to happen.

This morning Otis was an Indian. He was thinking of a movie he had seen last Saturday at the Kiddie Matinee at the Laurelwood Theater. Instead of walking through the snow on the sidewalk, he slipped from tree to tree. When he had crept silently through the forest for a block, he saw Ellen and Austine ahead of him. He stopped being an Indian and became a boy again. He began to run.

Ellen looked over her shoulder. "Here he comes," she cried, as she grabbed Austine's hand and started to run.

Otis ran after the two girls. He did this nearly every morning on the way to school. Sometimes Otis ran as fast as he could. Other times he ran just fast enough to keep the girls running. After all, he did not want to catch them. He just wanted to tease them. Especially Ellen.

But this morning Otis did not chase the girls all the way to school. They had run only a block when Austine's brother Bruce cut through a vacant lot and caught up with them. Otis noticed he was wearing his Boy Scout uniform under his leather jacket.

"Hey, what are you kids running for?" Bruce called to his sister and her friend.

The girls stopped and Otis slowed to a walk. "He's chasing us," Austine panted.

"Him?" asked Bruce scornfully.

"Yes," said Ellen. "He chases us every morning."

"What would he do if he caught you?" Bruce asked.

Otis saw the girls look at each other. They didn't know. All three were silent while he walked past. He was tempted to yank Austine's hair ribbon as he went by, but he decided he'd better not with Bruce there.

Bruce said, "He wouldn't do anything!"

Otis thought this over as he continued down the street. What *would* he do if he caught them? He didn't know either. He guessed he would have to think of something. Now that there was snow on the ground, he might wash their faces.

Then he heard Bruce say, "I'll tell you what. You chase him."

Startled, Otis stopped and looked back. Ellen and Austine were staring at each other in surprise. Such an idea had never occurred to them. They giggled.

"Go on," urged Bruce. "I'll watch you."

With Bruce to protect them, the girls began to run. Otis stood his ground an instant and then he

began to run too. There was no telling what two girls might do if they caught him.

"That's it," yelled Bruce. The girls ran faster, their feet scrunching in the snow.

Otis ran faster too. That old Boy Scout, he thought, as his feet pounded through the snow and he unzipped his jacket to cool off. Probably thinks he's done his good deed for the day. I'll fix him. Otis made up his mind to let the air out of Bruce's tires as soon as the snow melted and he rode his bicycle to school again.

To Otis's embarrassment, the girls, protected by Bruce, chased him all the way to school. Of course, everyone on the school grounds saw him. They left their snow men and snowball fights to watch.

"Hey, Otis," yelled Stewy. "What are you running for?" Everyone laughed.

"What's the matter?" yelled a boy, throwing a snowball at him. "You scared of a couple of girls?"

Otis didn't know what to do. He was running because he didn't know how to stop.

"You go that way and I'll go this way," he heard Austine say, as they ran into the schoolyard.

They're surrounding me, thought Otis. Now what am I going to do? He turned and ran to the right. He nearly bumped into Ellen. He ran to the left. Austine was ahead of him. She reached out to grab him but he dodged away from her. There was Ellen again.

Otis tried to dodge a second time, but he was too late. Ellen grabbed his collar. With a quick twist of his body he wrenched himself out of her grasp. He felt something give and saw the top two buttons of his shirt pop out into the snow. Otis glared at Ellen. "Now see what you've done."

Then the bell rang, and the breathless girls left Otis and went into the building. He heard them giggling about the way they had made him run.

Several boys gathered around Otis and laughed.

"Jeepers, letting a couple of girls chase you," George said.

"Aw, keep quiet," muttered Otis, looking down at his shirt. Quickly he pulled it together at the neck, but he was not quick enough.

"Hey, fellows!" Stewy whooped. "Did you see his undershirt? It's pink!"

"Aw," growled Otis, taking hold of the rabbit's foot on his zipper and zipping up his jacket.

"Pink underwear! Whoever heard of a boy wearing pink underwear?" someone wanted to know.

"It isn't really pink," said Otis.

"It is, too," contradicted Stewy. "I saw it."

"Well, it isn't supposed to be pink," protested Otis. "My mother put one of my glow-in-the-dark socks in the washing machine by mistake, and it faded and dyed everything pink. Sheets and towels and everything."

The boys laughed. Otis's explanation did not

change the color of his undershirt. They were not going to let him forget it.

And they didn't, either. Word soon spread around Rosemont School that Otis was wearing pink underwear. Otis took off his jacket in the cloakroom and went to his desk, where he fastened his shirt with a paper clip and slid down in his seat with a scowl on his face. Every boy in Room Eleven stopped at his desk and asked to see his pink underwear. The more Otis thought about it, the more he didn't like being chased. He didn't like losing his buttons, either. And it was all Bruce's fault for not minding his own business. And that Ellen . . . she'd be sorry!

As the boys and girls struggled out of boots, sweaters, jackets, coats, scarves, ear muffs, caps, and mittens they babbled not only about Otis's pink underwear, but also about the snow and the coasting they were going to do after school. They could hardly wait.

Mrs. Gitler had to clap her hands several times for attention. Then she said, "I know we are all excited about the snow and are eager to go coasting, but that does not mean we may neglect our schoolwork. Let's forget about the snow until school is out."

The class exchanged glances. What a silly thing for Mrs. Gitler to say. How could they forget about the snow when it was falling past the windows this very minute?

"Who has something to share with the class during Telling Time?" Mrs. Gitler asked.

Stewy shot up out of his seat. "Otis Spofford wears pink underwear," he announced in a loud voice, and sat down.

Instantly the class was in an uproar. Otis felt himself turn red. He glared at Stewy and drew back his fist to show Stewy he had better look out.

Mrs. Gitler rapped on her desk with a ruler. "Stewart, I'm disappointed in you. You know that is not the sort of thing we talk about in Telling Time. The class is not interested in the color of Otis's underwear."

That's what she thinks, thought Otis.

Ellen was next to tell something to the class. "This morning the milk was frozen in the bottles on our front porch. The cream stuck way up above the tops of the bottles and the caps were sitting on top of the cream."

"That's nothing. Ours has been that way for a week," said Tommy. The rest of the class agreed, and Ellen looked embarrassed because she had not noticed the frozen milk sooner.

"That means the temperature went down to freezing, doesn't it?" Mrs. Gitler remarked, before she called on George.

"Last night my dad took my brother and me in the car over to Laurelwood Park to see if the lake had frozen over. There was ice all over it except in the very middle where the ducks swim around, so it can't freeze. Some men from the fire department were looking at it. They said if it was as cold last night as it has been the last few nights, the ice would be thick enough to skate on." George looked pleased to have brought this news to the class.

Boy, I'm sure going to the lake, thought Otis, as an excited murmur ran through the class. Not every winter was cold enough for outdoor skating.

"Thank you, George," said Mrs. Gitler. "From what Ellen told us about the frozen milk we know that we had freezing weather last night. How many of you plan to go skating?"

Half the boys and girls raised their hands. Otis and the rest of the class buzzed with plans for skating and coasting until Mrs. Gitler told them to take out their arithmetic books.

Otis enjoyed the air of excitement, but Mrs. Gitler had a difficult time teaching arithmetic. Because of the weather, the class had to stay in during recess. Mrs. Gitler said it was like being in a room with thirty-five wild Indians.

After lunch, when everyone had again scrambled out of boots, sweaters, jackets, coats, scarves, ear muffs, caps, and mittens, half the class complained about being hit by snowballs by the other half. Everyone was saying either "I did not," or "You did, too," until Mrs. Gitler clapped her hands, blew on her pitch pipe, and had everyone sing *Jingle Bells*. That helped for a few minutes. The rest of the afternoon, while Mrs. Gitler tried to teach, the boys and girls looked out of the windows to see if more snow was falling or at the clock to see how much time was left before they could be out in it. Mrs. Gitler looked at the clock too, and said she was glad when the last period of the day came and she could tell the class to take out their readers.

Reluctantly, Otis took *With Luke and Letty on the Oregon Trail* out of his desk. With a feeling of great dislike, he looked at the picture on the cover. Another couple of dopes, thought Otis. Boys and girls in readers were always dopes. They were always polite and they never used slang and they hardly ever did anything they shouldn't. Except for wearing old-fashioned clothes and saying "Yes, Pa," instead of "Yes, Father," Luke and Letty were just like all the rest. Dopes!

Yesterday the class had read about Luke and Letty crossing the North Platte River in their covered wagon. Nothing much happened. The wagon tipped a little and Letty said, "Oh, Pa, what will we do if the wagon tips over?" It didn't tip over, though. Otis thought that if he had written the story he would have dumped the whole bunch of them into the river and had them chased by a herd of buffalo besides.

With no enthusiasm at all, Otis turned to the next chapter. There was a picture of an Indian at the top of the page. That was a good sign. Something might happen in this chapter. If he had his way about it, the Indian would scalp old Luke and Letty and that would be the end of the reader.

Mrs. Gitler called on Stewy to read first. He read, without expression, " 'Look, Pa, Indians,' said Luke. 'Oh, Ma, what shall we do?' asked Letty."

Otis made a face. That was the way Luke and Letty always talked. It sounded even worse the way Stewy read. Well, he knew what he would do if Indians were coming after him. He'd grab a gun and get down inside the covered wagon where the Indians couldn't see him and then when they got close enough . . .

"Otis." Mrs. Gitler's voice broke into his thoughts. "You may read next."

Otis got to his feet. He wasn't sure where the place was, but he took a chance. "Uh . . . Letty climbed into the wagon to hide from the Indians while Luke helped Pa round up the cattle that followed—"

Mrs. Gitler interrupted. "Otis, I don't know where you have been, but the rest of the class have traveled to the top of the next page. Please begin there."

Otis continued. "Then Pa said, 'Do not be afraid. These Indians are friends of the white man. They bring us robes made of buffalo skins.'" Otis paused. How do you like that! he thought. Friendly Indians! Who wanted to read about friendly Indians?

"Go on, Otis," said Mrs. Gitler.

"But, Mrs. Gitler," objected Otis, "I thought the Indians went on the warpath and burned the pioneers' wagons and stuff. They do in the movies."

All the other boys nodded in agreement. George spoke up. "I went to the show Saturday and there was this Indian that—"

"Never mind, George," said Mrs. Gitler sharply. "Many of the Indians were friendly to the pioneers. Right now we are studying the reader, not the movies."

Most of the boys and girls in the class had seen the same movie. They, too, preferred movie Indians to reader Indians. The room buzzed with talk about the movie.

Stewy said, "And there was this Indian creeping up on—"

"Never mind," said Mrs. Gitler even more sharply, as she glanced at the clock. "You may continue, Otis."

But Otis had lost the place once more. He was thinking what he would do if he were an Indian. He could see himself covered with war paint, riding down on a wagon train.

Mrs. Gitler sighed and looked at the clock as if she were afraid this day might last forever. "That will do, Otis. Ellen, you may continue reading the story."

Ellen stood up, but she did not have a chance to read. The buzzer sounded on the telephone that connected Room Eleven with the principal's office. The class was silent, because it wanted to hear what Mrs. Gitler said.

"Thank you. I'll be right down," she said into the telephone. Then she turned to the class. "Boys and girls, Mr. Howe wants me to come to the office for a few minutes. While I am gone, you will continue reading to yourselves. Remember, I'm putting you on your honor."

This meant the class was supposed to behave, even though no one was watching to see that they did. And they did behave until they were sure Mrs. Gitler was safely out of hearing. Then, except for a few unusually good girls who went on with their reading, the room began to hum with activity. Several children went to the window to see how much snow had fallen since lunchtime. Tommy threw an eraser across the room at George. Gary appointed himself a sentry at the door to watch for Mrs. Gitler's return.

Austine ran up to the front of the room and sat

at Mrs. Gitler's desk. "Boys and girls, I'm waiting," she said, the way Mrs. Gitler did when she wanted the class to be quiet.

"Austine Allen, I'm going to tell on you," said Linda.

Austine made a face at Linda and ducked as Tommy threw an eraser at her.

Otis was still thinking about those friendly Indians in the reader. It wouldn't be any fun to be a friendly Indian. If he were an Indian, he would be unfriendly. Chief Otis, the unfriendly Indian, that's what he was. He jumped out of his seat. "I'm an Indian," he announced. "I'm on the warpath." He put one hand behind his head and held up two fingers to look like feathers. The other hand he patted over his mouth while he warwhooped.

"You better keep quiet or they'll hear you in the next room," someone said.

Otis whooped more softly. Then he did a sort

of war dance. "Me heap big chief," he said. "Me chase 'um paleface."

"Heap Big Chief Lose-Place-in-Reader," scoffed Stewy, and pegged him with an eraser.

Otis went on with his war dance. Some of the other boys joined him and pranced up and down the aisles whooping softly.

Stewy ran around the chalk rail, gathering erasers for ammunition. He passed them out to the other boys, who pelted the Indians with them. The Indians dodged these bullets. Two who were hit clutched their chests and fell to the floor, where they died before they got up and grabbed some chalk to throw back at the palefaces.

Otis looked around for a weapon. A pair of snub-nosed scissors lay on Mrs. Gitler's desk. He snatched them and held them like a hunting knife. "Paleface squaw better run or big chief scalp 'um," he said to Austine, who was still sitting at the teacher's desk.

"I'm not a squaw," Austine giggled. "I'm a
beautiful maiden."

The boys hooted at this, and Austine let Otis
chase her back to her seat.

"Austine," whispered Ellen, "be careful. Mrs. Gitler will be back any minute." Then she went on reading, and as she read she tugged at a lock of hair to make it grow faster.

Now I'll have some fun, thought Otis, as he watched Ellen tug at her hair and look so neat and clean and well behaved. He had not forgotten about those two shirt buttons. Advancing with his scissors, he said, "Big chief scalp paleface maiden."

Ellen glanced up from her book. "Otis Spofford, you stop it," she said, and went on reading.

"Ugh," answered Otis, disappointed at not getting a rise out of Ellen.

"Woo-woo," whooped the braves. Ellen continued to ignore Otis.

"Paleface maiden better run for her life," he ordered, trying not to laugh. That ought to make her forget her old reader.

"Otis Spofford, stop being silly," said Ellen, and turned a page.

Otis flipped her book shut and danced down the aisle and up the other side of the row of desks.

"Big Chief Pink Underwear," Ellen scoffed, as he passed her desk. Then she and Austine began to giggle.

Otis held up the scissors threateningly. "Take it back!" he demanded. Maybe Ellen did pull the buttons off his shirt, but she was not going to call him Big Chief Pink Underwear and get away with it.

Ellen pulled away from the scissors. "I take it back," she cried.

She better, thought Otis, as he started to prance away from her desk. He guessed he'd showed her.

Then Ellen took her right hand out from under her desk and held it up with two fingers crossed. "I fooled you," she said. "I had kings when I took it back."

The class laughed. Otis could see everyone was delighted to have Ellen get the better of him. He felt his face grow hot and he quickly grabbed a handful of Ellen's hair.

Ellen halfway stood up in her seat. "Ouch," she protested. "Otis Spofford, you stop it. You're pulling my hair."

"Do you really take it back?" Otis raised the scissors. What would it feel like to cut off a big hunk of hair?

Ellen tried to jerk her hair out of his hand. "Ouch!" she said again, as silence fell over the class.

Otis opened the blades of the scissors. He knew the class waited breathlessly. They thought he wouldn't dare . . . or would he?

He watched Ellen's horrified stare as the scissors came closer and closer. Much as he had always wanted to cut someone's hair, he wouldn't really cut Ellen's. He would just tease her a little.

Then, out of the corner of his eye, Otis saw Austine spring from her seat. "You leave Ellen alone," she shouted. "You're not going to cut her hair!"

Otis twisted out of Austine's grasp. "Ouch!" shrieked Ellen. "You let go of my hair!"

"Aw, he won't cut your hair," Stewy said. "He'd be scared to."

Oh, I would, would I, thought Otis. I'll show him. Without taking time to think, Otis brought the scissor blades together on Ellen's hair. They cut easily through a few hairs on the edge of the handful he held. It was a wonderful feeling.

Ellen, frozen with horror, did not move, but she gasped, and her gasp made Otis hesitate.

"Well, go on," said Stewy. "I thought you were going to scalp her. What are you waiting for?"

Stewy needn't think Otis was going to back out now. He couldn't. Anyway, now that he had started, he had to know what it felt like to cut

that hair. With all the strength he had, he forced the blades together on the thick locks in his hand. Triumphantly he held up a brown handful. "Me scalp 'um," he announced.

Then Otis saw Ellen staring at that handful of hair, her eyes round with horror. She felt the side of her head with her hand. "My pigtails!" she whispered, as if she couldn't believe what had happened.

Otis stopped being an Indian and stared too. Ellen's pigtails. Why, she had been waiting months for her hair to grow long enough to braid. What had he been thinking of, anyway? It had all happened so fast.

Otis looked uneasily around the silent classroom. Why didn't somebody say something? Why did everyone sit there staring at him?

Then Stewy said, "Boy, you've sure done it now."

No matter how guilty he felt, Otis wasn't going to let Stewy know he was the least bit worried about what he had done. He held a lock of Ellen's hair under his nose and turned his lip up as far as it would go. Twirling the ends of his mustache he grew more and more uncomfortable. Something was wrong. Nobody laughed. Nobody even smiled.

Otis turned to Ellen again. He waited for her to tell him to stop, to stamp her foot, or burst into tears. Instead, she stared back at him, her cheeks flaming.

Suddenly Otis noticed that all the others were bent over their readers. Then he saw Mrs. Gitler and Mr. Howe in the doorway. As he felt Mrs. Gitler's angry glance take in everything, his lip uncurled and Ellen's hair fell to the floor. Otis shifted his weight from one foot to the other. Why didn't Ellen burst into tears and tell Mrs. Gitler all about it and get it over?

Instead, Ellen turned on him so fiercely that he stepped back. "Otis Spofford!" she shouted, in front of Mr. Howe and everyone. "You're going to be sorry for what you've done!" Then she flung herself angrily into her seat and bent over her reader.

Otis had never known Ellen to behave this way. He looked at the two red spots that flamed in her cheeks and at the hair that fell against one side of her face and stuck out rough and jagged on the other. If only there were some way he could stick her hair back on!

Mr. Howe spoke quietly. "Otis, you may come with me to the office."

Trying to walk with just enough swagger to make the class think he wasn't worried, Otis started toward the door, where the teacher and the principal were standing.

Mrs. Gitler no longer looked angry. "Well, Otis," she said, as he followed Mr. Howe into the hall, "I have a feeling that this time you're going to find out what come-uppance means."

And as Otis glanced back at Ellen's jagged hair and flaming cheeks, he had a feeling Mrs. Gitler was right.

CHAPTER SIX

Otis and Ellen

OTIS SPOFFORD could not think of a time when he had been as uncomfortable as he was this Saturday morning. He was shivering in his undershirt, waiting for his mother to iron him a shirt so he could go skating at the lake. Mrs. Spofford always put off ironing shirts until the last minute. This time Otis couldn't wear a T-shirt, because she had painted the kitchen cupboards yellow, and somehow both his T-shirts had been used for paint rags.

Worse than being cold, however, was the thought of yesterday—how he cut Ellen's hair, and the lecture the principal gave him, and how he squirmed on his chair while he had to listen to Mr. Howe telephone Mrs. Tebbits and tell her what had happened to Ellen's hair.

Otis listened to his mother's wet finger sizzle against the iron and watched her pull a shirt out of the clothesbasket and unfurl it over the ironing board. "Gee, Mom, can't you hurry?" he begged. "I want to get to the lake before the crowd." Otis did not say he was especially anxious to get to the lake because this was his only chance to skate. The principal had told him he would have to stay after school every day for the next week.

Mrs. Spofford pushed the iron rapidly back and

forth while Otis rubbed his arms to keep warm. "Otis," she said, "I want to have a talk with you."

Otis was not surprised. Grownups were always wanting to have talks with him. This time he knew what it was about. Mrs. Tebbits had phoned his mother at the dancing school about Ellen's hair. Now he was going to catch it all over again.

"It's about Ellen," said his mother.

"Yeah, I know," answered Otis.

Mrs. Spofford continued. "When Mrs. Tebbits came to the studio to pay for Ellen's dancing lessons last week, she said Ellen is upset because you chase her. I don't think that is a very nice thing to do, do you?"

"But she runs," said Otis, kicking at a fluff of dust on the floor to hide his surprise. Something was wrong. Maybe his mother hadn't heard about Ellen's hair. "If she didn't run, I couldn't chase her, could I?"

"Just the same, Mother would rather you didn't.

If you upset Ellen, she might stop taking dancing lessons and we can't afford that. We need all the pupils we can get."

"Aw, she won't stop taking lessons. She's always talking about being a famous ballerina when she grows up. Anyway, I stopped chasing her." Otis did not bother to tell his mother why he had stopped. He wished Mrs. Tebbits *had* phoned about the hair. He wanted to get it over with so he could forget the whole thing.

"That's a good boy." Mrs. Spofford handed Otis his shirt. "There are still some wrinkles in it, but I can't spend any more time on it or I'll be late for my class."

Otis hurriedly put on his shirt, which was still warm from the iron but damp at the collar and seams. " 'By, Mom," he called, as he put on his jacket, picked up his skates, and hurried out of the apartment. He wasn't going to let Ellen's hair spoil his skating. There was plenty of time to worry when he came home. He ran down the street past the Spofford School of the Dance and the Payless Drugstore, to the bus stop.

When Otis got off the bus he ran two blocks to the park, where he waded through the snow to the edge of the lake. There he sat on a bench to take off his boots and shoes and put on the old skates someone had given him. With three pairs of socks they were a pretty good fit.

Otis left his boots under the bench and, after knotting the luminous laces of his shoes together, hung them on a bush. There was no danger of anyone's taking his shoes by mistake—not with a green lace in one and a pink lace in the other. Anyone at Rosemont School would know those shoes belonged to Otis Spofford. As for his boots, they were plainly marked with his name in indelible pencil. Mrs. Gitler had seen to it that there would be no mix-ups over boots and rubbers in her cloakroom.

Otis, who practiced at Iceland whenever he had enough money, was a fairly good skater. Eagerly he stepped on the ice and started around the lake. It seemed strange to skate without organ music, but it was fun to be outdoors and watch snowflakes drift down on the ice and the trees around it. Around and around the lake he skated. His troubles over Ellen's hair no longer seemed important. Otis was enjoying every minute, but he could hardly wait for some of the other fellows to arrive. Then he would really have some fun.

Otis tried darting in front of skaters to see how close he could come without hitting anyone. Here there was no attendant to tell him to stop, the way there was at Iceland. Ahead of him was a girl on white figure skates, who was moving timidly along the edge of the lake. Her ankles wobbled and she held out her hands, ready to grab a bush if she started to fall. Otis noticed that she had short brown hair that curled around her red ear muffs.

Otis darted in front of the girl and then looked over his shoulder to see what was happening. The curly-haired girl started to fall. As she grabbed a bush, Otis saw who she was. He was so surprised that his feet flew out from under him and he sat down on the ice so hard he bit his tongue.

The girl with the curly brown hair was Ellen Tebbits!

"Otis Spofford, you leave me alone," said Ellen furiously, as she clung to the bush. "I've had enough of you!"

Otis sat on the ice and stared. "Your hair," he gasped. "What did you do to your hair?"

Ellen glared. "My mother cut it off even and gave me a home permanent, so now my hair will be curly while I wait for it to grow long enough for pigtails," she answered, as Austine coasted across the ice to her side.

Austine pretended not to see Otis. "Come on, Ellen," she said. "There are some people around here we don't want to have anything to do with."

"But just the same," Ellen said fiercely to Otis, "you're going to be sorry for what you did. You've been teasing me ever since you came to Rosemont School and I've had enough! You're just a . . . a pest, that's what you are!"

Otis recovered from his surprise and got to his feet. "Aw . . ." he muttered, not wanting to let on he was already sorry. So that was why Mrs. Tebbits hadn't phoned his mother. She had been busy curling Ellen's hair.

Ellen's brown eyes flashed. "And you know something else?" she asked. "I'm not scared of you any more." She stepped forward, put her hands on Otis's shoulders, and pushed as hard as she could.

Otis staggered backwards and sat down hard on the ice a second time. The wind was knocked out of him. Unable to speak, he stared up at Ellen in amazement. Ellen Tebbits pushing him! Ellen, of all people.

"So there!" said Ellen.

"Yes, so there!" repeated Austine, joining hands with Ellen. "So there, tee-hee!" Ignoring Otis, the two girls skated shakily away along the edge of the lake.

Dazed, Otis stared after them. He would not have been surprised if Austine had pushed him, but Ellen . . . When he finally got to his feet, something made him glance over his shoulder. Ellen and Austine, no longer shaky on their skates, had circled the lake and were behind him once more.

Maybe I better sort of disappear in the crowd, Otis thought, but before he had a chance, Austine spotted him. She scooped up a handful of snow, wadded it into a ball, and threw. Otis ducked too late. The snowball slammed against his shoulder. Some of the skaters in the crowd laughed. I bet that old brother of Austine's taught her to throw, Otis thought crossly.

"Pie-face," said Austine haughtily, as she and Ellen skated by. "You just wait."

Otis skated unhappily around and around the lake. He was careful to stay out of the girls' way. Skating wasn't so much fun after all. Maybe he should leave and go coasting instead. Then Otis caught a glimpse of George and Stewy through the crowd. Eagerly he skated toward the two boys. Now he would have some fun. "Hi, fellows," he said, dragging one toe on the ice to slow himself down. "Gee, I thought you'd never get here."

"Hi," answered George and Stewy.

They sound sort of funny, thought Otis, but he said, "Come on, I'll race you round the lake."

Stewy looked at him coldly and said, "Why don't you go find somebody to pick on? Somebody littler than you."

"Yes," agreed George. "Some *girl*."

For a minute Otis was unable to believe what he heard. "But . . ." he said weakly. He couldn't find words to finish the sentence. Without so much as a backward glance, George and Stewy skated off into the crowd.

"Aw, hey, fellows . . ." Otis called, but no one heard. Dazed, he stood and let the crowd skate around him. Gee whiz, didn't he have any friends left? Just because he cut off a hunk of Ellen's hair when he didn't really mean to, did the whole world have to turn against him? And Stewy—why, it was old Stewy who egged him on. If it hadn't been for Stewy, he wouldn't be in this mess at all. Some friend he turned out to be!

"Out of the way, stupid," said a skater.

Still dazed, Otis made his way through the crowd to the edge of the lake. Now he had to avoid not only the girls, but George and Stewy as well. He guessed he wouldn't skate around the lake any more. Halfheartedly, he tried skating backwards, but it wasn't any fun alone.

While Otis was trying to think what to do, he caught the sound of his name above the scrape of skate blades on the ice. It was Linda speaking to two girls he did not know. "See that boy over there? His name is Otis Spofford," Otis heard her say. "He's in my room at school and yesterday he did the awfulest thing. There's a girl who's been trying to grow pigtails for months and he . . ."

Otis moved away. He didn't want to hear how terrible he was. Couldn't anybody see he hadn't meant to cut Ellen's hair? Things just happened too fast, was all. Otis practiced skating with his hands in his pockets awhile, but he didn't enjoy it. A light flurry of snow fell and the wind grew colder. Otis knew it was time to start home for lunch. He might as well. He wasn't having any fun, anyway.

But when Otis went to the bench to get his shoes and boots, he found Ellen and Austine there ahead of him. Their noses were red and their fingers looked numb, as they unlaced their skates and put on their shoes.

Otis started to slip away before they saw him. Then he suddenly changed his mind. Why should he be scared of a couple of girls? Maybe he had done something he shouldn't, but what could they do to him besides push him and throw a few snowballs at him? Nothing, that's what!

"Frizzletop!" Otis yelled at Ellen. There! That ought to show them he wasn't worried.

The girls ignored him. Ellen leaned over to find

her boots in the pile that had collected under the bench. Otis could see snowflakes clinging to her new curls.

"Hey, Frizzletop, leave my boots alone," Otis yelled, and clapped his damp gloves together to warm his hands. Otis Spofford worried by a couple of girls? Ha! What a joke!

"Nobody wants your old boots." Ellen pulled two pairs of red rubber boots out from under the bench and gave one pair to Austine.

Otis skated around in a circle. Brrr, it was cold. He wished the girls would hurry up and leave, so he could put on his shoes and go home.

When Otis looked at the girls again, Ellen was whispering in Austine's ear. Austine looked surprised and then delighted, as she nodded her head. Both girls glanced at Otis and giggled.

Now what are they up to? Otis wondered, as he looked down at his feet and tried to cut a figure eight on the ice. He lost his balance on the first stroke and when he looked up again he was horrified at what he saw.

Ellen was holding his shoes by the pink and green laces. Austine held one of his boots in each hand. "Good-by, Otis," they both called, as they waved his footwear. Then they turned and started across the snow.

"Hey!" yelled Otis. "Come back here." He skated so fast to the edge of the lake that he tripped and almost fell. "Hey, you! Come back here," he called.

Giggling, Ellen and Austine waved the shoes and rubber boots.

Of course, they were just teasing him. They wouldn't dare go off and leave him without his shoes. Otis decided to go along with their joke. "So long," he called. That would show them he wasn't worried.

"So long," answered Austine cheerfully.

"You'll be sor-ree," Ellen sang out, as she smiled

and waved the scuffed Oxfords with the gleaming laces.

There was something about the way the girls acted that made Otis afraid not to grin. "Aw, come on. I know you're just joking," he said.

"Oh, no, we're not," said Ellen and Austine at the same time. Once more they turned and started out of the park. By that time a group of skaters, including Stewy and George, had gathered to watch Otis and to laugh at him.

"I guess they're going to fix you," called Stewy.

"Boy, this is going to be good," said George, and the boys laughed.

Otis stepped up onto the bank of the lake. "Hey, Ellen," he pleaded. "Come on, cut it out."

"Frizzletop to you," Ellen answered over her shoulder. Then she and Austine shrieked with laughter. The rest of the skaters laughed too, but Otis didn't think it was funny. It wasn't funny at all.

There was nothing for Otis to do but go after the girls. He ran out into the snow on his skates, calling, "Hey, Ellen, wait a sec."

The girls paused to let Otis come closer. Ellen dangled the shoes by the laces. Austine, who was wearing a boot on each hand, clapped them together.

Just as Otis thought they were going to let him catch up, the girls turned and ran. Otis ran faster, but they had a head start. Besides, they were not wearing skates. Maybe they would stop teasing and give back his shoes when they came to the edge of the park. They could hardly expect him to run after them on his skates on the sidewalks, which had been cleared of snow.

At the edge of the park, the two girls paused and waved. "Yoo-hoo, Otis," they sang out before they ran on.

Through the shrubs that bordered the park, Otis could hear two pairs of boots clomping on the cement. A short cut was his only chance. He pushed his way into the bushes. Branches caught at his clothes and snapped in his face. Snow showered over him. He burst out onto the sidewalk in front of the girls.

"Look out, there he is!" Ellen shouted, and both girls turned and ran the other way.

Otis did not care how dull the cement was making his skates. He was going after those girls and he was going to catch them. "You just wait," he yelled as the steel blades on his feet ground against the sidewalk. Running on skates made his toes hurt and his legs ache.

Ellen paused long enough to stick her tongue out at him. Otis scooped up a handful of snow, squeezed it into a ball, and hit her between the shoulders. Bits of snow clung to her coat.

At the intersection, the girls crossed the street with the green light. Otis reached the corner just as the light turned to yellow and then to red. As he waited for it to change, he saw George and Stewy running down the street toward him. They *would* have to turn up now, thought Otis miserably. Now I'll never hear the last of this.

As the signal changed, George and Stewy caught up with Otis. The girls, standing on the opposite curb, waved the shoes and boots. "Yoohoo, Otis," they yelled. His shoelaces gleamed brightly through a flurry of snow.

"I guess they fixed you." George was laughing

so hard that he could hardly get the words out.

"And old Ellen Tebbits, too." Stewy laughed even harder. "Boy, I wouldn't miss this for anything."

Otis wasn't going to listen to any more of the boys' guffawing. He stepped out of the snow and ground his way across the street. The two boys followed.

"Hey, Ellen," Otis called desperately. "I'm sorry about your hair."

"It's too late now," yelled Ellen.

The girls began to run again. Then Austine tripped and fell. As Ellen paused to help her to her feet, Otis nearly caught up with them. Now I've got you, he thought grimly.

"Hey, Ellen," yelled Stewy. "Throw!"

Two shoes and two boots sailed over Otis's head. He jumped and tried to snatch them out of the air, but the girls had been too quick for him. He landed on the sidewalk with a jolt that turned both his ankles. George and Stewy scrambled to pick up his footwear.

"Ellen, Austine, run!" ordered Stewy. The girls ran. Then the two boys dashed past Otis and caught up with Ellen and Austine. The girls took back Otis's shoes and boots and ran on down the street.

George and Stewy turned back toward the park. Otis glowered as they passed him once more. "You're some pals!" he grumbled.

"Remember the bullfight?" asked George.

"And remember Spud's flea?" asked Stewy.

Otis had no answer.

"We're going to get a couple of hot dogs and then go skate some more," said George. "Too bad you don't have shoes so you could come with us."

"Go on, eat your old hot dogs. I don't care," muttered Otis, but he knew he did care. Anyway, he thought, those girls can't run all the way home. I'll catch them at the bus stop. I'll fix them yet.

Even though it was difficult to run in rubber boots, the girls managed to stay half a block ahead of Otis. When they turned the corner by the bus stop, Otis thought, Now I'll get them. He decided the first thing he would do would be to wash Ellen's face with snow. That Ellen Tebbits! She'd be sorry.

As Otis limped around the corner, he stopped and stared. The bus was pulling out from the curb. Ellen and Austine were not in sight.

"Hey, come back here," Otis yelled at the bus. He could not believe the girls had actually left him to go home on the bus without his shoes. He looked around to see if they had hidden his shoes and boots. Then he looked after the bus. There in the back window was the very thing he did not want to see. Ellen was waving his shoes. Austine was waving his boots.

Otis made a good hard snowball and threw it after the bus. How his legs ached. Leaning against the bus-stop sign, he glumly made a design in the dirty snow with the point of his skate. Girls! he thought bitterly. And Ellen Tebbits, of all people. And just because they were best friends, Austine had to help her. When he caught up with them, he would not only wash their faces, he would put snow down their necks.

Otis began to worry about getting on the next bus. Probably the driver wouldn't let him on wearing skates. Well, he couldn't very well take them off. He turned down his pants cuffs and stepped into a pile of snow so his skate blades wouldn't show.

When the bus came, Otis's fingers were so cold that after finding the dime in his pocket he dropped it on the floor, where it rolled under the driver's seat. "I'll get it," said Otis quickly, but the driver had already bent to pick it up.

When the man straightened up with the dime in his hand, he looked at Otis, shook his head, and said, "I suppose there's some reason why you're wearing skates on the bus?"

"Isn't it all right?" asked Otis. "They aren't very sharp. See?" He grabbed the fare box to steady himself and held up one foot.

"I see," said the driver, as the passengers began to laugh.

"Is there a rule that says I can't wear skates on the bus?" Otis wanted to know. The driver had to let him ride. He couldn't walk home with his toes hurting and his legs aching this way.

"The only reason there isn't a rule is that nobody ever thought anyone would want to wear skates on a bus. It takes a boy to think up something like that." The driver shook his head again. "Now sit down on that seat behind me and don't step on anyone."

Ordinarily, Otis would have been pleased to stir up a little excitement on the bus, but now all he wanted to do was rest his aching legs a few minutes. He wiggled his toes and wondered how many blisters he had. His toes were so numb with cold he couldn't tell. Maybe his feet were raw and bleeding.

"Boys!" muttered the driver, as he closed the door and shifted gears. "Boys!"

On the way home Otis worried about his shoes. What would Ellen and Austine do with them? They were the only shoes he had for wearing to school in cold weather. He pictured himself going to school on his skates. For a minute he thought it might be a good idea. He would like to see Mrs. Gitler's face when he walked into her room on skates. Then he thought how his legs ached and how he wouldn't be able to play dodge ball during lunch period. No, it wasn't worth it. He would rather wear shoes to school.

When Otis got off the bus at his corner by the post office, he thought he heard giggles. The two girls popped out from behind a sign that said

Uncle Sam needs you. Rosy and breathless with laughter and cold, they started running again. This time they were not running very fast.

Now I'll catch them, thought Otis. And I'll *scrub* their faces with snow. But when he started to run, he found his legs were so tired they would no longer move the way they were supposed to. He felt as if he were running in slow motion.

"Oh, Ellen," he heard Austine say, as she stopped to lean against a tree, "I've run so much my side hurts."

"So does mine," panted Ellen, "but we can't let him catch us now." In the cold air, Otis could see Ellen's breath coming from her mouth in quick puffs.

Around the corner they went, past the Payless Drugstore and the entrance to the Spofford School of the Dance. Valerie Todd Spofford was just coming out of the building.

"Hello, Mrs. Spofford," panted Ellen and Austine, as they ran past.

"Hello, girls," said Mrs. Spofford. "My, you're in a hurry, aren't you?"

Austine nodded, and pointed toward Otis, who was trying desperately to put on a burst of speed.

"Otis Spofford!" exclaimed his mother. "I am disappointed in you. What did I say to you this morning about chasing the girls?"

"But I'm not chasing them," Otis protested, as the girls slowed down to listen.

"Why, Otis, I just saw you." Mrs. Spofford sounded shocked.

"He is, too, chasing us," said Ellen. "He chased us all the way home." The girls began to giggle.

"I was running after them, but I wasn't *chasing* them." Otis did not suppose his mother would see the difference.

"Now, Otis," said Mrs. Spofford. Then she saw his skates. "Otis Spofford, is that any way to treat a perfectly good pair of skates?"

"No, but . . ." Otis saw Ellen and Austine walking rapidly down the street. Now how was he going to explain to his mother? "No, but . . ." he started again.

His mother interrupted. "Otis, I don't know what gets into you. Now run along home while I pick up some groceries for lunch." Valerie Todd Spofford turned up the collar of her coat against the cold and hurried down the street.

Girls! thought Otis grimly, as he limped along on his aching legs. And now his mother said he was chasing them. Well, they could keep his old shoes. He didn't care. He probably had so many blisters on his toes he couldn't get them on anyway. Maybe he would have to stay home from school. Then they would be sorry.

Otis felt more and more sorry for himself. The more he thought about himself, the sadder he became. Half frozen. No shoes. Blisters on his feet. Picked on by girls. Misunderstood by his mother. And hungry besides.

When at last Otis limped up the street to his apartment house, the only person in sight was Bucky, who was sitting on the front steps eating a cupcake. There was a lopsided snow man near the steps.

Wearily, Otis threw himself down beside Bucky. "Hi," he said, looking hungrily at the cupcake. Just his luck to run into Bucky. Now he would have a lot of explaining to do about his skates. Little kids always asked so many questions.

"Hi," said Bucky, digging into the pocket of

his snow suit. "Want a cupcake? I saved one for you."

"Sure." Otis took the crumbled cupcake. He took a big bite. Mmm, chocolate with nuts. He felt better almost at once, but, boy, how he ached! And his feet!

"How come you're wearing skates?" Bucky wanted to know.

"Because." Otis's answer was muffled by a mouthful of cupcake. What would the kids at school say when they heard about the good joke Ellen played on him? And it was a good joke, he grudgingly admitted. She sure did get even with him for cutting her hair. He just hoped she brought his shoes back before Monday. Otis started to lick the frosting off his fingers so he could unlace his skates.

Suddenly Ellen and Austine popped around the corner of the apartment house. "Why, there's Otis Spofford." Austine pretended to be surprised.

"Fancy meeting you here," said Ellen sweetly.

Now what? thought Otis, as he glared at the girls.

"We found a pair of shoes and a pair of boots at the lake and we wondered if they were yours," said Ellen. Both girls went off into a gale of giggles.

"Otis," said Bucky, "how could you forget your shoes?"

This made the girls scream with laughter.

"Aw, cut out the funny business." Otis was too tired to think about washing the girls' faces with snow. All he wanted to do was sit right where he was. "You give me my shoes."

"So long as you said you were sorry you cut my hair, you can have them if you promise to stop teasing me," said Ellen.

"And cross your heart and hope to die and stew and fry," added Austine.

Otis was silent. Girls!

"Well, come on, Austine," said Ellen. "I guess he doesn't want his shoes back."

"I guess not," agreed Austine, starting to walk away.

"Hey, wait a minute," begged Otis. "I've got to have them." Then he thought of something. Quickly he thrust one hand behind his back.

"Are you going to stop teasing me?" Ellen demanded.

Otis didn't want to say it. "O.K.," he muttered.

"And cross your heart and hope to die and stew and fry," repeated Austine firmly.

" 'S m' heart, hope to die 'n' stew 'n' fry," Otis mumbled.

The girls handed him his shoes and boots. Then they burst into a fit of giggles and started down the street.

"Are you really going to stop teasing Ellen?" Bucky wanted to know.

Otis grinned and said, "I'll still tease her all right, but after today I won't tease her as *much*." He looked at the girls, whose shoulders were shaking with laughter. "Hey, Ellen!" he yelled. "Look!" The girls turned and Otis held up his right hand with two fingers crossed. "I had kings all the time!" he shouted.